Praise for Jennifer Sturman's Rachel Benjamin mystery series

The Pact

"Sturman is as adept   ch
for a good man as sh   ,
making *The Pact* a
and readers who e
with a d

—*Booklist*

"Why is this debut so thoroughly enjoyable?
Perhaps it's because Rachel is such a
winning detective: she sifts through clues at the
reader's pace and does so with wit and pluck.
The novel's *mise en scène*—successful, attractive
Ivy League graduates at a lakeside mansion—makes
for escapist pleasure, and well-placed cliffhangers, a
careful distribution of motives and unexpected twists
promise readers light, satisfying suspense."
—*Publishers Weekly*

The Jinx

"*The Jinx* is a welcome sequel to *The Pact*,
Sturman's debut novel, and the author has populated
Rachel's world with characters quirky enough to be
entertaining, but not defined by their quirks."
–*Akron Beacon Journal*

"Rachel returns for another smart and saucy adventure
in sleuthing and romance in Sturman's second fresh,
funny, and fabulously amusing chick-lit mystery."
—*Booklist*

JENNIFER STURMAN

THE KEY

A RACHEL BENJAMIN MYSTERY

RED
DRESS
INK
TM

THE KEY

A Red Dress Ink novel

ISBN-13: 978-0-373-89603-5
ISBN-10:   0-373-89603-4

www.RedDressInk.com

Printed in U.S.A.

This book is dedicated to Anne Coolidge Taylor

Thanks to Laura Langlie, Selina McLemore,
Margaret Marbury and the team at Red Dress Ink
for their help and advice, and to my family and friends
for their encouragement and support.

THE
KEY

chapter one

I was having my favorite type of dream, a flying dream, when the phone rang.

I opened one eye, testing to see if this was part of the dream. But in my dream the skies were blue and lit by golden sunlight. In my bedroom, it was dark, and freezing, since my new roommate liked to sleep with the windows wide open, even in March and even in Manhattan. And the phone was still ringing.

Peter mumbled something unintelligible and pulled the duvet over his head. I thought about doing the same, but surely nobody would call in the middle of the night unless it was important. I reached out for the phone.

"'lo?"

"Rachel. Glenn Gallagher here."

This had to be a joke. "What time is it?"

"Almost six. Listen, I need you in the office. We don't have much time to get ready."

"Ready for what?"

"I'll tell you when you get in. See you in an hour."

"But it's Satur—" I began to say before I realized I was talking to a dial tone.

I was still half-asleep, so my reaction was somewhat delayed. It was nearly five seconds before I'd collected myself sufficiently to say the only appropriate thing that could be said in such a situation.

"You asshole!"

Peter gasped and shot into a sitting position. I'd spoken more loudly than I'd intended. "And a good morning to you, too." Even in the dark, I could make out the silhouette of his sandy hair.

"You look like Alfalfa."

"Excuse me?"

"From *The Little Rascals.* You know, the one with the piece of hair that stuck straight up. He sang."

"'I'm in the Mood for Love.'"

"Uh-huh. He had a crush on Darla."

"And that makes me an asshole?"

"No. Who said you were an asshole?"

"You did. Just now."

"Oh. I wasn't talking to you."

"Good to know, I guess." He settled back into the pillows and reached for me. "So who were you talking to?"

I snuggled into his embrace. Despite the Arctic chill to the room, his body radiated heat. "Glenn Gallagher.

But he didn't hear me call him an asshole. He'd already hung up."

"Ah."

"Yes. Ah."

"Who's Glenn Gallagher?"

"The new guy Stan Winslow brought in."

"And why was he calling us in the middle of the night?" Even as I answered Peter's question I was marveling at the unfamiliar use of "us." I'd lived alone from the day I graduated college until the previous week, and I still wasn't accustomed to the first person plural being applied in reference to my household. Our household.

"He said he needs me in the office. In an hour. Actually, more like fifty-five minutes at this point."

"Do you think he knows it's Saturday?"

"Probably."

"And do you think he knows we were going to sleep in? And have a nice leisurely brunch and read *The New York Times*? And then figure out where I can put all my stuff?" Peter's worldly belongings had arrived from San Francisco a few days ago, and stacks of unopened cardboard cartons now occupied every available square foot of the apartment.

"I doubt he gave it that much thought."

"Why do you do this again?"

I sighed and detached myself from Peter's arms. The rug was cold beneath my bare feet. "Because this is how you make partner at an investment bank."

"By letting assholes order you out of bed in the wee hours on weekends?"

"If I keep it up, one day I'll get to order other people out of bed in the wee hours on weekends."

"Something to look forward to."

"Go back to sleep. I'll call you later, when I know what this is all about. Maybe I can rescue at least part of our day together."

But I wasn't too confident about that.

By Monday morning, the only thing I was confident about was that I wanted Glenn Gallagher dead.

My brain was fried and my thoughts scattered from too much caffeine and not enough sleep, but I did know with absolute clarity that I despised Glenn Gallagher and would be delighted to see him die a slow and painful death.

My firm, Winslow, Brown, had lured Gallagher from a competing bank six months ago, bringing him in as a senior partner and lavishing him with an enormous corner office and matching expense account. He'd been putting together leveraged buyouts for close to thirty years, and while LBOs were no longer as fashionable as they'd been in the junk-bond fueled eighties, Gallagher seemed to be doing just fine, judging by the addresses of his homes on Fifth Avenue and in Bridgehampton.

Regardless of his impressive real estate holdings, it hadn't taken long for him to become the most hated man at Winslow, Brown—no easy feat in a place where there were a lot of hated men and even a few hated women. By the end of his first week he'd terrorized enough junior bankers to earn some interesting nicknames, including Adolf and Saddam.

Gallagher had learned late on Friday that Thunderbolt Industries, a Pittsburgh-based defense contractor, had chosen Winslow, Brown as its advisor on a management buyout. He hadn't wasted any time scheduling a meeting with Thunderbolt's CEO for Monday morning, which left just the weekend to get ready. Meanwhile, I wasn't sure how my name had ended up at the top of the staffing list, but I'd lost this particular game of Russian Roulette without even realizing I was playing. I'd spent most of the past forty-eight hours in the office with Jake Channing and Mark Anders, the other unfortunates who'd been shanghaied into working on the deal.

The "team" had gathered in Gallagher's office for a final prep session. He had called another 7:00 a.m. meeting but hadn't sauntered in until half past, and he was now attending to a few personal matters before we began. First we were treated to a conversation, on speakerphone, between Gallagher and his lawyer regarding his ex-wife's complaints that he was behind in child support. Gallagher earned more in a year than most people earned in a lifetime, and the fees he paid his lawyer probably far exceeded the sums he coughed up for the basic care and feeding of his daughter, but he apparently was not the sort to open his checkbook on behalf of others without the threat of legal action.

The next call was to a tailor to complain about the imperfect fit of a custom-made suit, which seemed futile, at best. Gallagher could spend every penny he made on his clothes, and he still wouldn't be much to look at. He had the physique of a scarecrow, with stooping shoulders and sallow skin. What hair he had was a mousy shade, and the cut did nothing to disguise the way his ears stuck out.

I stole a glance at Jake, who rolled his eyes in shared exasperation. Like me, he was a vice president, although slightly more senior, and while he'd transferred only recently from the Chicago office, we'd quickly become friends. But I still hadn't figured out how he always managed to look as if he'd just come from a GQ photo shoot. Today was no exception—his blue eyes were bright and every blond hair was in place—nobody ever would have guessed that he was running on only a few hours of sleep.

Mark, on the other hand, took nondescript to a new level: brown-haired, brown-eyed, neither short nor tall, and in no danger of being mistaken for a male model. Still, he seemed like a decent guy, unassuming and mild-mannered, and as the junior-most person on the team he'd more than pulled his weight over the hellish weekend.

Gallagher reached for one of the pencils he kept in a silver mug on his desk and rammed it into an electric pencil sharpener. He sucked on the newly sharpened point as his tailor stammered a response. Gallagher let him get a few words out before he snatched up the receiver, uttered an impressive string of expletives, and slammed the phone down.

"Where is it?" he barked.

Jake handed him a neatly bound sheaf of papers.

"This had better be an improvement over the crap you faxed me last night."

"We've made a lot of progress since then," Jake assured him. He'd worked with Gallagher before and was one of the few people around who seemed unfazed by his complete lack of interpersonal skills. I, on the other hand, was gripping my chair's armrests so tightly my knuckles were white. In an industry notorious for badly behaved people, Gallagher was in a class by himself.

He flipped through the pages, giving an occasional grunt. The presentation was flawless—we'd double- and triple-checked every detail—but he almost seemed disappointed when he didn't find even a single typo.

"I guess it will do," he said grudgingly. "Now, here's the drill. Nicholas Perry, Thunderbolt's CEO, will be here at ten. I do the talking. You guys keep your mouths shut unless I ask you a direct question. And you'd better know every number, every fact in here, backward and forward. There's big money riding on this. Got it?"

"Got it," I said. "But I was wondering about something."

Gallagher narrowed his eyes in an expression that made him look even more like a ferret. "Wondering about what?"

"Well, Thunderbolt—" I winced every time I said the word—what sort of phallo-centric moron would name a company Thunderbolt? "—just doesn't seem like an obvious candidate for a buyout. Its revenues have been declining, and the union's making trouble so its labor costs are likely to increase, and—"

"Your point?" asked Gallagher. "Get to the point already."

My grip on the armrests tightened yet further. "The point is that a buyout will add a lot more debt to Thunderbolt's balance sheet. The company's interest payments will sky-rocket, and I don't see how it will cover them."

An LBO is sort of like buying an apartment by making the smallest of down payments and taking out a huge mortgage, all based on the assumption that you can generate enough money renting out the apartment to cover the mortgage payments. In this case, it was unclear that you could count on the tenant paying his rent on time. Or that you'd even be able to find a tenant in the first place.

Gallagher gestured impatiently toward the dozens of Lucite deal mementos lining his credenza. "See those? Each one represents a successfully executed LBO."

Successfully executed, maybe, but more than a couple of the Lucites bore the names of companies that no longer existed, victims of a crushing debt load.

"I've been in this business a long time," he said. "I know what I'm doing. So, why don't you do your job, and I'll do mine?"

"I was just—"

"Enough already! Nick Perry and I go way back—I've known him since Princeton. This deal is ours, and I'm not going to let anything screw that up. We do the work, we collect our fees, and everybody goes home happy. Can you get that through your pretty little head?"

Unbelievable. He'd actually said, "pretty little head."

Pick your battles. That was what my mother always told me. Good advice, certainly, but not necessarily easy to follow. I opened my mouth to speak again but he cut me off.

"Dahlia!"

Dahlia Crenshaw, Gallagher's secretary, hurried in. "Yes, Mr. G.?"

"I need some goddamn coffee in here. Pronto."

Dahlia did not point out that technically her workday wouldn't begin for another hour. Nor did she point out that getting coffee was not in her job description, however politely she was asked to fetch it. Instead, she smiled sweetly. "Sure thing, Mr. G."

Jake and I exchanged another look. Gallagher had brought Dahlia with him from his previous firm, and the office gossips were convinced that, in the tradition of bosses and secretaries throughout time, the two were having an affair. That Dahlia bore more than a slight resemblance to Jessica Simpson only helped fuel the rumors. And putting up with Gallagher, day in and day out, was just too much to ask without some fringe benefits. Not that it was clear how an illicit relationship with Gallagher would be a fringe benefit.

"We're done here," he announced, dismissing us with a wave of his hand. "Meet me in the conference room at ten with copies."

I was following Jake and Mark out when I heard his voice behind me.

"Rachel, not so fast." I turned, and Jake turned with me. "Just Rachel," said Gallagher. He motioned for Jake to leave and shut the door, which he did, but not before shooting a commiserating glance my way.

"Courage," he said under his breath.

Gallagher put his feet, shod in well-shined Gucci loafers,

on his desk. "We need to have a little talk," he said, rolling a pencil between his palms.

"All right," I said in an even voice, admiring my own self control. It was probably a good thing that I was so tired; if I had more energy, I would still be too angry to speak, given his cavalier dismissal of my concerns about the deal, not to mention the "pretty little head" comment and everything that had come before it.

"This is a warning. I don't want to hear any more crap from you. Understand?"

"Yes."

"Because if you make trouble on this, I'll be happy to find another VP to work on the deal. I wasn't exactly thrilled to have you on the team in the first place."

"Why's that?" I asked. This time it was a struggle to maintain my even tone. I was one of the hardest working bankers in the department, and the other partners thought highly of me.

"I demand a lot from my teams. Girls like you—they've got other things going on. Work doesn't come first for them." The only thing missing was a lascivious up-and-down once-over, but he'd gotten that out of the way on Saturday, along with a thinly veiled and equally lascivious proposition.

I felt my shoulders stiffen. I pulled myself up to my full height, painfully conscious that this was only five feet six inches even with the aid of high-heeled pumps, and bit back a number of retorts that would put this pathetic, rodentlike excuse for a human being in his place.

Bonus, I reminded myself. Partnership.

"I don't think you'll have a problem with either the quality or the quantity of my work," I said.

"As long as we understand each other."

"We do. We definitely do."

chapter two

The one advantage to being among the few female bankers in the department was that I could always retreat to the ladies' room when upset—or, in this case, enraged. It was a relatively safe place to get my emotions in check; the only other people I was likely to encounter were the administrative assistants on the floor. They were a sympathetic group, but it was still a relief to find I had the room to myself.

I ran shaking hands under cold water from the tap and bent forward to splash some onto my flaming cheeks. No matter how level I'd managed to keep my voice, my face always betrayed me. I didn't need to look in the mirror to know that two spots of crimson were staining my usual late-winter pallor. I averted my gaze—I didn't want to see my reflection; it would only drive home the overwhelming feeling that I was trapped, running toward a goal that proved ever more elusive. How many times had I stood before this same sink, trying to calm myself after a disappointment or confrontation?

Get a grip, I told myself. Don't let him get to you.

But how dare he question my abilities? Much less my commitment? I'd been at it for eighty hours a week for years, but that weasel assumed, just because I was female, that I was some kind of dilettante, that I'd wandered into Winslow, Brown by accident and was sticking around on a whim. If anything, I was as ambitious as any of the men at the firm, perhaps more so—I'd dealt with so much *crap*—to borrow one of Gallagher's favorite words—that I was determined to make partner, if only to prove that I was better than most of the men with whom I worked. Another few months and that partnership would be mine, or so the department head, Stan Winslow, had assured me. Not only would my income soar, I finally would be in a position to start doing things the way I wanted to do them.

I took some more deep breaths, exhaling slowly as I waited for my anger to subside and for my fantasy of beating Gallagher over the head with a blunt object to work its cathartic magic. After a minute or two, my hands were still trembling, but just a bit, and Peter's ring shone bright and reassuring on my finger. I took a final deep breath, squared my shoulders, and headed through the door.

I crashed immediately into Dahlia Crenshaw.

"Ooof," I said.

"Oh! I'm sorry. Are you okay?" I didn't have time to answer before Dahlia burst into tears.

"I'm fine," I said, leading her back into the safety of the ladies' room. "But you're clearly not. What's going on?"

She sank onto one of the stools in front of the vanity. "You have to ask?"

"Gallagher?"

"I hate that man."

"He's a rat," I agreed. "But you can't let him get to you." Easier advice to give than to take, as I well knew, but suggesting that she fantasize about beating her boss over the head with a blunt object seemed unprofessional, at best. I crossed to a stall, ripped a length of toilet paper from the roll and handed it to her. She wiped her eyes and blew her nose.

"Why don't you quit?" I asked.

"I'd leave in a heartbeat if I could, but the money's good and the firm pays for my night classes—I'm getting my nursing degree, did you know? I can't afford to quit. After all, it's only my pride I'm sacrificing here." She said this with a bitter smile, and fresh tears began streaming down her cheeks, streaked with black from her running mascara.

I perched on the counter beside her. "Is there anything I can do to help?"

Dahlia shook her head. "You could kill him for me," she joked with false bravado.

I laughed. "I'd kill him for myself. He sure hasn't won me over. I don't know how you can stand it."

"I can't," said Dahlia in a forlorn voice, the bravado gone. She turned to the mirror and began dabbing at the tracks the tears had left. "So much for waterproof mascara."

"No mascara could stand up to these working conditions."

"Working for Gallagher is bad enough. But it's even worse knowing that everybody thinks we're having an affair."

I felt a wave of shame wash over me. That was exactly what everybody thought, including myself until a moment ago.

I was a bad liar, so I didn't even try to convince Dahlia that the rumors weren't out there. "Look, people are so desperate for a bit of intrigue, they'll believe anything. But that's a rumor that can be squashed."

"I hope so. I mean, it's not like he didn't come on to me when I first started working for him, but I nipped that right in the bud, and I'm too good at my job for him to get rid of me. But how could anyone think I'd have anything to do with him? And why does he always have to be such a jerk, yelling and obnoxious? Didn't anyone ever teach him any manners?"

"He does seem to have missed out on the common courtesy gene. I wish I knew how to solve that one."

"You can't," said Dahlia. She sighed. "Sorry to unload on you like this."

"No problem. I've had a few nervous breakdowns in here, too."

"You? Impossible. You're always so poised. Calm, cool, and collected."

If she only knew. "Hardly. Anyhow, are you feeling better?"

"Better? Not really. But I'll be fine." She dabbed at her face a final time and rose from the stool. "And I should get back. This new deal seems to have him particularly worked up. Do you know that two different people have already called from Thunderbolt for a team list?"

"They probably want to send some more materials over," I said, but I had to stifle a groan as I followed Dahlia out the door. The last thing we needed was another influx of documents and spreadsheets. It was hard to believe it was only Monday. And it was depressing, too. An entire week ahead and not a break in sight.

Little did I know what the week held in store.

chapter three

My own assistant, Jessica, was at her desk outside my office when I returned.

"So," she said, "judging by the stack of stuff you left for me, I'm guessing that you were here all weekend, weren't you?"

"Yup."

"And this was your first weekend with your new *room-mate,* too. When are you going to get a life?"

"At this rate, never."

"And how is Il Duce?"

"Don't ask."

"You're the boss."

"Please, no Tony Danza jokes. I'm running on empty here."

"I had a feeling about that. I left a little fuel for you in your office."

"You are my new best friend."

"You might want to wait and see what I brought you before getting rid of your old best friend."

I was incredibly lucky to have Jessica as my assistant. An aspiring actor, she was absurdly overqualified for her current job with a degree in drama from Yale, and she'd saved my skin on more than a few occasions. Unfortunately, she was also a bit of a health nut. Instead of the bagel and cream cheese I'd been hoping for, the bag she'd left on my desk contained a distressingly wholesome-looking bran muffin and some carrot juice.

I reached into the small refrigerator under my desk and pulled out a can of Diet Coke. Carrot juice just wasn't going to cut it this morning. I picked up the phone, cradling it against my shoulder and dialing Jake's extension with one hand while I popped open the can of soda with the other. I probably could have walked over to his office, but it was on the other side of the floor and that seemed like too much work.

"Hey," he said.

"Hey. So, are we ready?"

"I think so. Mark's dealing with the copies."

"He's a machine."

"Yes, and he's our machine, thank God."

"Good point."

"So, what did Gallagher want with you?"

"Nothing much. Just to warn me to keep the thoughts in my pretty little head to myself."

He chuckled. "Don't let him get to you." That seemed to be a recurring theme today.

"Who, little ole me? Worry my pretty little head with silly details about a silly ole deal?"

"Cute, Scarlett."

I switched back to my own accent. "Let's just say, if Gallagher suddenly dies a mysterious death—"

"We'll know who to bring in for questioning."

"Exactly."

"Rachel," he said. "Seriously. Do you want me to say something to him? Or to somebody else?" Jake had come into my office on Saturday shortly after I'd slapped Gallagher's hand from my arm and told him that no, I had no interest in joining him for lunch at an intimate restaurant he knew nearby. I'd still been sufficiently upset that it hadn't taken much coaxing to get the story out of me.

"What could you say?" I asked. "Everything he's said and done can be explained away. It's all too subtle, and it's all his word against mine. And he's a rainmaker—he brings in more fees in a month than I bring in all year, so I think I know where the partners' loyalties lie."

"I don't care how much money he brings in. He shouldn't be allowed to get away with this sort of thing."

"I'll just deal with it, and once I make partner, I'll never have to deal with it again."

"Well, let me know if you change your mind…."

"Thanks, Jake. I appreciate it."

"No problem. See you at ten?"

"At ten," I confirmed and hung up the phone. "Pretty little head, my foot," I muttered, washing the words down with a swig of soda.

I turned to where I'd left my briefcase on top of the credenza, unlatching it and drawing a battered spiral-bound notebook from an inside pocket.

The notebook contained a hundred sheets of ruled paper, but it was already more than half-filled, which wasn't surprising given that I'd been making regular entries for years. I opened to a fresh page and printed the date at the top. Then I quickly summarized my interaction with Gallagher, "pretty little head" and all. I tried to describe it objectively, which was challenging given the rage still coursing through my veins. I wrote steadily for several minutes before pausing to look over my account. Satisfied that I'd captured everything important, I flipped through the preceding pages.

The previous entry was from Saturday afternoon and described the first incident with Gallagher. The page before that held a description of my most recent meeting with the partner assigned to be my "mentor." He'd insisted on conducting my last performance review over drinks and had swilled down three Glenlivets while I nursed a seltzer and fought off his attempts to steer the conversation toward my love life, rather than my professional development.

The notebook was my version of an insurance policy, started at the urging of my friend Luisa, a lawyer. I wanted to succeed on my merits, but it hadn't taken long to realize that there was a lot more than merit to succeeding on Wall Street, especially as a woman. If I ever found myself getting the shaft for reasons that I suspected had more to do with my gender than anything else, I had a detailed record of all I'd put up with over the years.

None of my experiences met the legal definition of sexual harassment, but as a whole the handwritten pages told a compelling story.

I'd returned the notebook to my briefcase and was cranking through the e-mails overflowing my in-box when the intercom buzzed. "Peter's on line one," Jessica told me.

"Thanks, I'll take it," I said and picked up the phone, still typing with my free hand. "Hi."

"Good morning."

"Not so far."

"That's the attitude, Sparky."

"What's up?"

"I wanted to check in and see if maybe you could sneak out for a nice romantic lunch today."

I hadn't told Peter about Gallagher's far less welcome invitation—it would only upset him, and he was already concerned about how hard I'd been working—so he couldn't have known the unfortunate associations lunch invitations held for me just then. Nor was there any way I was going to be able to sneak out for a nice romantic anything. In fact, sneaking out for a decent night's sleep was probably going to be a problem, and I told Peter as much.

"That bad, huh?" Peter ran a tech start-up, and while he worked hard, he was his own boss and set his own hours. It wasn't always easy for him to understand how little control I had over my own schedule.

"Just business as usual. Listen, I'll call you when I know how things are shaping up. Maybe we can try to grab a late dinner?"

"That would be great. I feel like I see less of you than I did before we lived together."

"I'm sorry," I said lamely. "But this deal can't last forever." At least, I certainly hoped it couldn't. "I'll talk to you later?"

"All right," he agreed.

My other line was ringing, and I checked the caller ID. "That's Jake. I've got to run."

I'd hung up before I realized Peter was still talking. "Love you—" he was saying.

I felt guilty, but only partly because I'd had so little time for Peter of late.

The other part was because I was annoyed that I felt guilty. A nasty little voice in my head was saying that Peter should know well enough by now what my job was like, that he couldn't expect me to drop everything whenever he called. Just because he had a key to my apartment didn't mean that he had a key to my entire life.

And the very existence of that nasty little voice made me feel all the more guilty.

chapter four

Jake, Mark and I took the single flight of stairs up to the designated conference room a few minutes before ten. "Where should I sit?" asked Mark nervously, setting the stack of bound presentations on the table. Client meetings were still pretty new to him—he'd joined the firm only a few months ago after graduating early from an undergraduate finance program, opting to start work immediately rather than use the extra time to travel or take a few electives.

"I wouldn't just yet," I advised. "I'm sure Gallagher has some master plan about how he wants to position us." Like kneeling at his feet, awaiting his next command. Jake smiled as if he knew what I was thinking, and he probably did.

Gallagher arrived a moment later, deep in chummy conversation with his companion—Nicholas Perry, presumably. Next to Perry, Gallagher looked especially mousy, as Perry was well over six feet and bore a striking resemblance to George Hamilton, albeit dressed in a pin-striped suit rather than a Zorro costume.

Jake stepped forward and introduced himself, shaking Perry's hand.

"Hello, Jake," Perry said.

"And this is Rachel Benjamin and Mark Anders." I had the feeling that Jake didn't trust Gallagher to get the names of his minions right and had preempted the introductions accordingly.

"Nice to meet you." He turned to Gallagher. "This is quite a group you've assembled here, Glenn." There was something oily about his tone, or maybe it just seemed that way because he looked so slick, from his shining tasseled loafers up to his sleekly barbered hair.

Gallagher shrugged—he saved his chumminess for old college pals—and glanced at his Rolex. "Ready to get started?"

"Let's do it," agreed Perry with a glance at his own Rolex.

Sure enough, Gallagher did have strong ideas about seating. In my case, it was at the end of the table farthest from Perry. For once I was happy to be marginalized.

"We've run the numbers," he told Perry as we took our places. "And the bond department is raring to go—we should be able to get this done in a couple of weeks."

"The faster the better," said Perry.

Gallagher began walking him through the materials we'd put together, with Jake, Mark, and I adding the occasional clarifying detail when called upon. The mechanics of the proposed buyout were fairly straightforward. Perry would purchase all of Thunderbolt's shares, financing a small part of the acquisition with fifty million dollars put up by his investor group. The remainder would be financed by bonds that Winslow, Brown would issue and sell. The bonds, in turn, would be backed by Thunderbolt's future earnings. Perry's investor group would then own a company worth five hundred million dollars after putting up only ten percent of its value.

It was risky but perfectly legal. And Winslow, Brown would net a cool three or four million dollars in fees for a few weeks' work, a healthy chunk of which would be deposited directly into Gallagher's pocket. It was good to be a partner, and especially good to be a senior partner.

"The only thing standing in the way is getting the new union contract signed. Did you wrap up the negotiations?" Gallagher asked Perry.

"We finalized everything over the weekend. Kryzluk, the chapter president, is a bit bull-headed, but the last thing he wanted was layoffs—he had to cave on benefits." He said this as if the decline in Thunderbolt's business was a plus, because it meant that the union had to yield on its demands to ensure that employees kept their jobs.

"Good," said Gallagher, who probably didn't spend much time pondering the fate of industrial laborers in a rust-belt town. Concern about that sort of thing would be a liability in his line of work.

As I listened, however, my unease only increased.

The whole deal smelled. As I'd tried to point out earlier, Thunderbolt was in bad shape. I didn't understand what

Perry or his anonymous co-investors were thinking—sure, the buyout would leave them in control, but with massive interest payments that the business couldn't support with its declining revenues.

When Gallagher paused to draw a breath, I spoke without thinking. "Are there any new contracts in the pipeline?" There must be a reason that Perry was so interested in owning the company—the man may have been slick, but I doubted he was stupid.

My question met with an awkward moment of silence. Then Perry turned to me, peering down the length of the polished mahogany table as if noting my presence for the first time.

"I don't think we need to worry about that," he said with finality.

Gallagher shot me a look that suggested he wished looks could, in fact, kill before changing the subject. A few minutes later he was chummily walking Perry down the hall to the elevators.

Gallagher had, of course, guaranteed Perry we'd have a revised set of numbers ready the next day, which meant that the rest of today and much of the evening were shot. I knew I couldn't face diving back into work without a short break—preferably one involving food—and Jake and Mark concurred. We agreed to reconvene in ten minutes for a quick lunch and headed downstairs to our offices.

I was at Jessica's desk, retrieving messages, when I heard

the panicked voice of Bert, the guy who manned reception, from across the floor.

"Ma'am? Ma'am? You can't go in there! I need to make sure you're expected—"

Jessica and I both turned to stare. The woman Bert was trailing ignored his protests. "Don't worry—I'll find my way, thanks."

She was average height and in her late forties, with the sort of face people describe as striking rather than pretty. Her dark hair was pulled back into a neat chignon, and she was wearing a smart navy pantsuit. We watched, curious, as she surveyed the open space of the floor, its center crammed with the low-walled cubicles that housed junior bankers and assistants, and the offices for more senior bankers lining the perimeter. Her eyes landed on Dahlia, seated at her station in front of Gallagher's own corner office.

"Hello, Dahlia," she called, threading her way through the maze of cubes.

"Naomi!" Dahlia's tone was surprised. Bert hesitated but seemed to take the greeting as proof of the intruder's legitimacy. With a shrug he retreated to reception.

"It's been a long time," said Naomi as she reached Dahlia. "I don't think I've seen you since Glenn and I signed the divorce papers. Is he in?"

"He had a meeting, but he should be back soon. I didn't know you were— I mean, do you have an appointment? Did he know that you were coming to see him?" Dahlia's polite smile began to give way to a more apprehensive expression.

"I think we're both aware that he would never agree to

see me in person." By this point the two women had the attention of everyone within earshot. There wasn't much drama during the course of a normal day at Winslow, Brown, but it looked like we were all in for an unexpected treat.

"Oh. He's not going to like this," said Dahlia.

Naomi shrugged. "Too bad, isn't it? Look, here he comes now."

"What the hell are you doing here?" The acoustics on the floor were pretty good, but it still may have been a strain for some of the eavesdroppers to make out what Dahlia and Naomi had been saying. Gallagher, however, could be heard easily since he was shouting.

"I was getting sick of my lawyer racking up fees talking to your lawyer," his ex-wife answered. She followed him into his office.

"He wouldn't be racking up fees if you weren't being so unreasonable."

"Unreasonable? Unreasonable?" Naomi's voice rose to match Gallagher's own, and while nobody could see them now, everybody could still hear them. "I hardly see how it's unreasonable to expect you to live up to your legal obligation to pay your daughter's tuition."

"I don't know why she has to go to that fancy school. What can they possibly teach her that costs thirty grand a year?"

"You listen here, Glenn Gallagher. If I'd known when I met you what a stingy schmuck you'd turn out to be, I would never have had anything to do with you. Beth is the one good thing that came out of our marriage, and I'm not going to let you stint on her education. It's the least you can do. I can't remember the last time you saw her. She probably can't, either."

Jessica looked up at me, bemused. "Stingy schmuck?" she mouthed. I shrugged.

"Can't we talk about this later?" Gallagher said. "I'm in the middle of something."

"No, we cannot talk about it later. I'm not leaving here without a check. And don't even try to cry poor. Your new apartment's the lead spread in this month's *Architectural Digest*. Little Annabel probably spent more on each square foot of that place than the school costs."

"There's no need to drag Annabel into this."

"I could care less about dear Annabel. All I want is for you to pry open your checkbook and write the check. Make it out directly to the school. If they don't get it in the next two days, Beth's going to lose her spot for next year. Or perhaps I should write a letter to the editor of *Architectural Digest?* I'm sure they'd be interested to learn all about how you managed to find the money to pay for your swanky penthouse but can't seem to scrounge up your daughter's tuition."

"I'll write the check. Just shut up already."

There was silence, and then the sound of a check being ripped from a ledger.

"This better not bounce."

"You're psycho. A real head case. Now get out of here before I call security."

"Gladly." Naomi reappeared at the door then turned back for one last parting shot. "You know, you'd be of more use to your daughter dead. Pull any more of this crap, and I'll kill you myself."

She walked calmly out of her former husband's office, and everyone who'd been listening hurriedly began shuffling papers or typing at their computers, feigning utter absorption in work. I stifled the urge to clap.

"I'm off," Naomi said to Dahlia. "But I have the feeling that he's not going to be much fun to deal with for the rest of the day."

The women's eyes met. Then Gallagher began yelling for Dahlia from his office.

chapter five

Naomi was still waiting for an elevator when I went out to the lobby a moment later to meet Jake and Mark. Listening to her let Gallagher have it had been almost as cathartic as if I'd done it myself, and it had definitely been more cathartic than my blunt-object fantasy. I wanted to thank her, but even I knew that probably wouldn't be appropriate.

She appeared preoccupied anyway, tapping her foot and checking her watch as she waited. My colleagues sat on the other side of the floor so had missed the entire scene—I was already looking forward to filling them in over lunch.

An elevator finally announced its arrival with a digital beep. The doors slid apart, framing another woman in the opening.

"Figures," I heard Naomi say under her breath.

The woman was about my age and roughly the same size, but that was where any resemblance ended. With her golden highlights and glossy manicure, not to mention the enormous diamond on her ring finger and matching studs in her ears, she was pretty much the illustrated dictionary definition of socialite-slash-trophy-wife. The Gucci jacket, Prada skirt, Manolo Blahnik heels, and Louis Vuitton purse did nothing to contradict the image, although I did find myself wondering if it was wise to mix so many brands at once. I also felt suddenly self-conscious. It must be nice to have the funds and leisure time to support such perfect grooming and over-the-top wardrobe selection. In fact, it must be nice simply to get enough sleep.

She and Naomi were standing face-to-face, and together they were blocking the elevator entrance, but it seemed rude to push past them.

The socialite-slash-trophy-wife heaved an exaggerated sigh. "Hello, Naomi."

"Well, hello, Annabel. You're looking coiffed. Here to see Glenn?" Naomi's voice dripped acid.

It wasn't just an image, then. This woman was, in fact, a trophy wife. Glenn Gallagher's trophy wife, to be exact. What could she possibly be thinking, marrying a weasel like him? But the outfit answered that question nicely—the jewelry alone likely added up to more than the annual income of your average top-tax-bracket American household.

Annabel sighed again and indicated a garment bag she had slung over one arm. The bag bore a Brioni logo, as if it needed a label to join the rest of her ensemble. "I'm bringing him his tux. We're going to a benefit tonight, and he won't have time to stop home to change."

"He's in a fine humor."

"Oh?"

"I have that effect on him. And I managed to separate him from some of his money. He never likes that much. Can I give you some advice, Annabel?"

"Do I have a choice?" she answered impatiently. She moved to step past Naomi, but Naomi moved with her. The elevator doors gave a whining beep in protest at standing open for so long.

"If you didn't already sign everything away in a prenup, which he probably made sure you did, get things squared away now. Especially if you're planning on having any little Annabels or Glenn juniors. Find a good lawyer and have him draw up some watertight contracts. Otherwise all you'll see once he's onto Number Three is half of whatever he made while you were married, and my guess is that he'll hide a lot of that away."

"Thank you for your concern, but I can take care of myself. Are you done now?" asked Annabel, trying again to step past Naomi. "These people are waiting for the elevator." She motioned toward our little group, which had been bearing witness to the entire scene with varying degrees of awkwardness. I thought I caught a flash of recognition in her eyes as her glance swept over us.

"Yes, I must get back to my office. Some of us work, you know. Besides, I wouldn't want to keep you from anything important. I know how busy you must be with all of that shopping and decorating to do. Goodbye, Annabel."

"Goodbye, Naomi," Annabel said, mimicking Naomi's tone. This time Naomi let her pass and stepped into the elevator, followed by Jake, Mark, and me. A small smile played over her lips as the doors slid shut.

We were all silent as the elevator descended. Personally, I was in awe. Naomi seemed to be completely comfortable saying whatever she wanted to whomever she wanted. And while Miss Manners most assuredly would not have approved, I couldn't help but be impressed.

The doors parted when we reached the ground floor, and Naomi strode off.

"Wow," I said.

"Good show," agreed Jake.

"You missed the first act." I filled them in on Naomi's showdown with Gallagher as we made our way to a nearby Burger Heaven. I'd chosen our destination; I was very much in need of protein, preferably accompanied by large quantities of French fries.

"It sounds like Wife Number One isn't exactly president of the Glenn Gallagher fan club," said Jake when we had settled in a booth and placed our order.

"I don't think that's a very happening club," I said.

Mark laughed, his first laugh in the three days we'd spent almost entirely in each other's company. I turned to him, glad to see some sign of personality. It would be nice if the guy loosened up—thus far, he'd been like a Stepford associate: focused, uncomplaining, and completely humorless.

"So, Mark, where are you from?" I asked.

"Me?" He took a sip of his soda. "New Jersey."

"Southern New Jersey or northern New Jersey?" asked Jake. I wondered how this could possibly matter. New Jersey was New Jersey as far as I was concerned.

"Southern."

"Then you're an Eagles fan, right?" said Jake.

My heart sank. I really hated sports talk, and it didn't help that I had no idea what sport the Eagles played.

"Yeah."

"Man, did you see their game against the Cowboys? During the playoffs?"

"Uh, no. I missed it."

"It was awesome." Jake started talking about the game, and I was able to ascertain that the sport in question was football. It was amazing how someone who was usually so engaging in conversation could embrace such a boring topic.

"What about the Eagles–Steelers game? Did you see that one?" Jake asked.

Mark looked relieved to be able to answer in the affirmative. "That was a great game."

They started talking about that game, and I tuned out. I couldn't possibly be expected to concentrate on a subject this dull when I was hungry. I perked back up when our food arrived, and I was pleased to find that the football discussion had run its course. They were now talking about work. This was only a marginally better topic, but it still trumped sports.

"You've been with the firm since January, right?" Jake was asking. "How do you like it?"

Mark picked up his burger. "I expected that the hours would be pretty brutal, and they have been, especially with this new deal. But I wanted to work on a buyout."

"Even with the Idi Amin of Winslow, Brown?" I asked.

Mark hesitated. "This is probably embarrassing to admit, but I was deciding between offers at a few different firms. When I heard that Gallagher had left Ryan Brothers to join Winslow, Brown—well, that made up my mind for me. In fact, I asked to be assigned to his next deal. I'd heard that working with him was sort of painful, but I thought it would be a good learning experience. He's kind of a legend in certain circles."

Circles of hell, I thought. Imagine *wanting* to work with Gallagher. In fact, following Gallagher to the firm? That was dedication. Or masochism.

"Then it's a dream come true?" asked Jake. He must have been thinking along the same lines as me; there was a teasing edge to his tone. But Mark looked uncomfortable, so I changed the subject.

"I have a question, Jake. Since you've worked with the guy before."

Jake turned his attention away from Mark. "Shoot."

"What's with Gallagher and the pencil thing?"

"What pencil thing?"

"Don't even try to pretend that you haven't noticed the pencil thing. When he sharpens an already sharp pencil and sucks on it? He must have done it six or seven times when we were in his office this morning."

He grinned. "Oh, that pencil thing."

"Yes, that pencil thing. He must go through a dozen pencils a day. And the sucking—it's disgusting. I don't even want to know what Freud would make of it."

"All that lead can't be good for him," volunteered Mark.

"Maybe he'll die of lead poisoning," I said, not bothering to disguise the hopeful note in my voice.

"I think they make them out of graphite now," Jake said. "It's funny, though. Do you watch *Forensic City?*"

"I love that show," I said.

"You do? Me, too," Jake said.

"I have the entire season's episodes on my TiVo, just waiting for the time to watch them all," I told him.

"Well, I don't think I'll ruin anything by telling you they had an episode a few weeks ago in which a guy who likes to chew on toothpicks dies from chewing on a poisoned toothpick."

"Interesting," I said thoughtfully. "Maybe we could slip some poison into one of Gallagher's pencils?"

"Should I be worried you're not joking?" asked Jake.

"I don't know. Would you be willing to help out?"

"For you? Anything." There was a gleam in his eye.

I laughed, but my cheeks felt strangely warm.

I decided to chalk up my reaction to hunger. "Could somebody pass the ketchup please?"

We lingered over lunch, and Jake talked about adjusting to life in New York after Chicago. "I lived here after business school," he explained. "That's when I first worked with Gallagher—I was an associate at his old firm. But my ex-wife was from Chicago and wanted to move back. Ryan

Brothers didn't have an office there, so I took the job at Winslow, Brown. But I was never a big fan of the Midwest, and it turned out that my ex-wife wasn't such a big fan of me. Once we split up, I hightailed it back to the East Coast."

I'd heard around the office that Jake was newly divorced after a short and unsuccessful marriage, but we hadn't talked about it much. He seemed glad to be back in New York except, of course, for the inevitable lament about real estate. "The prices are insane."

"I was lucky," I told him. "I bought my apartment years ago."

"Is there enough room for the two of you?" Jake knew that Peter had just moved in.

"It's a little cramped right now, but we'll figure it out," I said with false confidence. Given that every closet was already filled to bursting, I wasn't sure how this was going to happen. But I loved my home—its high ceilings and southern light and old-fashioned details—and I really didn't want to move. It was only since Peter had arrived that I'd realized just how attached I was to the place, and how much I'd gotten used to having my own space.

There had been a lot of snow over the weekend, but it had warmed up since then and the pristine white piles were quickly melting into dirt-colored slush. We had to navigate the pavement carefully on our way back to the office.

We missed the light at the corner of Madison and Fifty-first, but I was still scoping out the enormous puddle lapping at the curb, trying to figure out the best way across it, when the signal changed from the orange hand of "Don't Walk" to the striding white figure of "Walk."

"I've got you covered," Jake said.

"What—" I started to ask.

He grabbed me around the waist and hoisted me over his shoulder as if I weighed nothing, which most certainly was not the case, especially not after the meal I'd just consumed. He stepped easily over the puddle and continued across the street before depositing me on the opposite corner.

My feet were dry, but if my cheeks had felt warm before, now they were burning.

"Thanks," I said.

"Anytime," he grinned.

chapter six

A mountain of work waited for us in the office, but we were sufficiently fortified by lunch to get through it at an efficient pace. Still, it was well after nine by the time I let myself into my apartment.

I sensed instantly that something extraordinary was underway.

"Peter?" I called out, kicking off my shoes. I shrugged out of my coat and left it with my hat and scarf draped over one of the cardboard boxes in the foyer.

"In here," he answered.

"In where?"

"The kitchen."

"Why?" I asked. An old Van Morrison CD was playing on the stereo, and the apartment smelled strangely of food. My stomach reminded me with a rumble that lunch, however fortifying, had been a long time ago. I picked a path through the cartons that lined the hallway, heading toward the room in question.

"Why do you think?"

"Oh my God." I stood in the kitchen doorway, frozen with shock.

He was *cooking*.

"Lasagna all right with you? It seemed like a good choice for a cold night. It's almost ready. Here, let me pour you a glass of wine."

I struggled for words. "But—how? With what?" I didn't see any plastic containers from restaurant takeout, or even one of those orange boxes with the trusty Stouffer's logo. And the microwave was quiet. None of it made any sense.

"A casserole dish. The oven."

"It works?" I'd gotten a letter from ConEd years ago, warning that they were turning off the gas since it registered such little usage. I was pretty sure I'd never responded.

"Seems to." He handed me a glass of Barolo.

"I have a casserole dish?"

"It was a bit dusty, but I rinsed it off."

"But—but didn't you need spices and herbs and ingredient stuff?"

"There's a grocery store a couple of blocks away. They even deliver."

He was trying to act nonchalant, but he was clearly pleased with himself.

I put my glass down and wrapped my arms around him. "Will you marry me?"

"I'll give it some thought."

★ ★ ★

A few minutes later he banished me from the kitchen so that he could put the finishing touches on the meal. In the living room, I saw that he'd even set the small table. Place mats! Who knew I owned place mats?

I went to stow my briefcase in the tiny room that I used as a study and which technically elevated my apartment from a one-bedroom to a two-bedroom, although it had never been clear to me how it could possibly fit a bed when it could barely fit a desk and chair. The PC was on—Peter must have been using it—so I took a moment to check my personal e-mail account. My BlackBerry was like an extra limb, almost surgically attached to me and ensuring that I rarely fell behind on my work e-mail, but my home account tended to fill up.

Most of it was spam. The Internet was supposed to usher in a golden age of targeted, one-to-one marketing, but I refused to believe that I was the target market for penile implants. I sent message after message into the trash bin, clicking the mouse with increasing impatience and speed.

As a result, I nearly missed an e-mail from Luisa confirming drinks the following evening. In a fortuitous twist of events, all four of my college roommates were in New York this week, and we'd agreed to meet at the King Cole Bar at the St. Regis Hotel. I hit Reply All to caution them that I might be a bit late, but I resolved at the same time to make it out of the office at a decent hour. Gallagher and his deal would suck up every second if I let them.

The next and last e-mail also nearly missed being tossed

into the trash bin. And once I saw it, I almost wished I'd deleted it unread.

The subject line read Important. Of course, all of the Viagra ads claimed relevance and urgency, too.

But the return address was from manofthepeople@rsnd.net. Not the most legitimate-sounding address—it had a self-righteous rabble-rousing air to it—but it seemed more likely to be a real person than one of the randomly assorted strings of letters that most of the Viagra ads came from.

I clicked it open. The message was short, and cryptic.

Perry's dirty and so is this deal.
And they've done it before.

That was it. That was all it said.

chapter seven

The mouse suddenly felt like a burning coal, and I grabbed my hand away. I had the sinister sensation there was someone else in the room, a presence at my shoulder.

There was nobody there, obviously, and the dark night outside meant I could see nothing through the window but my own reflection, yet I still had the eerie feeling I was being watched. I yanked the shade down.

Then I read the e-mail again.

Perry's dirty and so is this deal.
And they've done it before.

The questions started flowing into my brain, but it took a couple of minutes before I could get over how creeped out I was to even articulate them, let alone begin to address them.

First, who was manofthepeople@rsnd.net? And why was he e-mailing me? Here, at home, on my personal e-mail account? How had he even found my personal account?

Second, how was the deal dirty? I wasn't surprised to hear somebody else thought so, too, but Man of the People had been a little stingy with the details.

Third, what, exactly, had they done before? And who were "they" supposed to be?

And fourth—well, I was back to Question One, Part Two—why was Man of the People e-mailing *me?*

"Rach?"

I shrieked. The entire concept of jumping out of one's skin made sense in a way it never had before.

"Sorry—I didn't mean to startle you. It's just that dinner's served."

I gaped at Peter.

"You remember dinner? The logical outcome of what I was working on in the kitchen? I know the entire dining-in thing is a bit novel and usually involves the delivery guy being buzzed up, but I promise there's food on the table."

"You need to see this," I told him.

"Can it wait? I don't want everything to get cold."

"I don't think so."

He came around to my side of the desk and leaned over my shoulder to look at the screen.

"You just got this?" he asked.

"Yes."

"On your personal account?"

"Yes."

"And you don't know who this Man of the People guy is or why he's e-mailing you, much less how he got your e-mail?"

"No."

"That's sort of creepy."

"It's very creepy."

Peter convinced me it would be unwise to discuss matters any further on an empty stomach. I plopped myself down at the table and allowed him to cut me a large slice of lasagna and top off my wine.

The food was delicious—much better than anything that came out of a box—but it was hard to give it the attention it deserved. Under Peter's careful questioning, I fleshed out the details of the Thunderbolt deal. We weren't supposed to discuss work with people external to the firm, but it was common knowledge that nobody obeyed that rule with spouses and significant others.

"I knew there was something wrong with this whole thing," I told him. "The company's practically in the toilet but meanwhile Nicholas Perry wants to do a buyout and Gallagher can't wait to help make it happen. I bet Gallagher's part of the 'they' somehow."

"At the very least, it shouldn't be too hard to find out what Perry's done before, or even if Gallagher was involved, too."

We left the dishes on the table and returned to the study. My desk chair wasn't really big enough for two, but we squished onto it together. It was probably a good thing I'd passed on the third helping of lasagna.

A page on Thunderbolt's own Web site providing biographies of its management team quickly yielded the answer to our first question. Several years ago, Perry had been CEO of another company, this one, like Thunderbolt, a major defense contractor. I recognized its name—Tiger Defense Enterprises—immediately. One of the Lucite deal mementos lining Gallagher's credenza bore its logo.

"What do tigers have to do with tanks or body armor or whatever this company makes?" asked Peter.

"Nothing. But a tiger is the Princeton mascot. That's where Gallagher and Perry met."

"You're joking, right?"

"It's better than Thunderbolt."

"Not by much."

Apparently the Tiger buyout, under Perry's leadership, had been very successful. Perry had not only added the Tiger to the company name, he'd implemented an impressive turnaround. The company then sold shares to the public at a price considerably higher than the buyout price. Perry's investor group more than tripled their money in a comparatively short timeframe. And Ryan Brothers, Gallagher's old firm, had handled both the original buyout and the offering when the company went public again. Perry was lauded as a management guru and left Tiger shortly after to join Thunderbolt as CEO.

"So they have done it before," Peter said.

"Yes. But I don't know what's dirty about it. If anything,

it's a textbook LBO. Take a failing company, buy it out, improve operations, and then sell it at a nice fat profit."

"Why don't we just ask him?"

"Who? Perry? Or Gallagher? I don't think either of them is going to be too receptive to my asking how their last joint venture was corrupt. They didn't seem too forthcoming when I tried to figure out what's going on with the deal they've got on the table now."

"No—not them. I meant your new friend. Man of the People."

I thought about this. It was one thing to talk things over with Peter, but it was quite another to engage in any sort of discussion with an anonymous correspondent. "If anything, I should probably be reporting him somehow. Communicating about a deal underway with somebody whose real name I don't even know is the sort of thing that falls into the strictly *verboten* category."

"Give me a few minutes to play around a bit with the e-mail address. Maybe I can find out more about who this guy is."

"How?"

"Rachel," he reminded me, "I'm sort of a geek."

"So that's why there are suddenly all of those *Star Trek* episodes on the TiVo."

"Worried that I'll record over your *Dawson's Creek* reruns?"

"I still get a rush every time Joey chooses Pacey over Dawson." I went to clear the table.

I rinsed the dishes and added them to the dirty pots and pans already in the dishwasher, another rarely used appliance. I rummaged under the sink, located a box of detergent that bore the logo of a long-since bankrupt grocery chain, poured some powder in, and selected the Power Scrub function.

The casserole was still half-full of lasagna, so I covered it with tinfoil and slid it into the refrigerator, noting with yet more astonishment that I actually had to rearrange one of the shelves to find room. Peter had bought more than the ingredients for lasagna. It was peculiar to see my fridge, which usually held only a limited selection of life's basic necessities—Diet Coke, white wine, and hot sauce—harboring a more usual assortment of groceries. There was actually butter in the butter compartment and eggs in the little indentations on the shelf alongside.

Peter was hunched over the computer when I returned. "Any luck?" I asked.

He sounded frustrated. "I'm not as much of a geek as I thought."

"That's probably not a bad thing," I said, perching on the arm of the chair beside him.

"All I could figure out is that he's using an e-mail resend service. It's pretty sophisticated, too. It's not a commercial service but a program that some hard-core techies set up for themselves."

"So you think he's a hard-core techie?"

"Maybe. Or maybe he's just friends with one. Either way, I can't get to any information about where the e-mail may have originated. Usually you can track down the various stops a message makes as it goes over the Internet, but the service he used erased all that. I'm afraid that the only way we're going to find out more is if you e-mail him back."

"I'm tempted to. But it's a bit of a quandary, in terms of professional ethics."

"If the deal is dirty, don't you have an obligation to find out how?"

"I think I'd be supposed to report it to Winslow, Brown's legal department or the Securities and Exchange Commission or something. But I don't even know it's dirty, and if I make a stink at the office without any proof, Gallagher will probably try to have me fired. He's already gunning for me."

"Maybe this guy can give you some proof. Would it be such a big deal to e-mail him and ask for more detail? You wouldn't be sharing any privileged information."

I was torn. The easiest thing to do would be to delete the e-mail as if it was another piece of spam, but I was too curious to do that. The by-the-book thing to do would be to show the e-mail to the firm's legal department, but I had no desire to incur further Gallagher wrath. And the tempting thing to do was to e-mail Man of the People back.

"You know, there are ways to cover your tracks," said Peter.

"You're like the little devil guy standing on my shoulder, trying to lead me astray."

"But I cook like an angel."

I had an idea. "Maybe I should call Jake and tell him about this. Get his opinion." Peter was used to the more rough-and-tumble startup world, without the bureaucracy and lawyers and regulatory oversight. Jake had a better sense of the context than Peter, and he would also have an appreciation for my concerns about things like Gallagher and the SEC.

"Jake? Jake from work?"

"Maybe he'll know what to do." I checked my Black-Berry for his cell phone number.

"Are you sure you can trust him?"

"Of course I can trust him." Jake and I had been friends even before we'd started working on this deal; several grueling days spent under Gallagher's command had further cemented that bond. Besides, I would never have told him about Gallagher's pass if I didn't trust him, and Jake had been kind and supportive, eager to rush to my defense while also being discreet.

But I couldn't explain all of that to Peter without opening up a whole can of worms I'd prefer to keep closed. "One mysterious e-mail and suddenly you're suspicious of everyone," I said instead.

"You barely know him."

"I know him well enough. He's a really good guy."

It didn't matter anyway. Jake's phone went straight into voice mail. I hesitated but didn't leave a message. It was late—he was probably asleep.

When I disconnected, Peter was looking at me, his fingers poised over the keyboard. And I was still torn.

"When you said there are ways to cover my tracks, what did you mean, precisely?"

chapter eight

I found myself back in Gallagher's office first thing Tuesday with a strange sense of déjà vu. Yet again, it was way too early for a meeting, and yet again, I hadn't gotten anywhere near enough sleep.

It had been close to one by the time Peter had set up a new e-mail account for me at a free service and we'd e-mailed Man of the People via the same resend provider he'd used. The e-mail—a simple and noncommittal request for more information—had been the easy part. It was the tracks-covering part that had taken so long. Peter had run a number of different programs he promised would erase all traces of Man of the People and our response from my computer. I'd never realized that paranoia could be so time-consuming.

"I feel like a criminal," I'd said.

"Look, this guy is probably a crackpot and it won't amount to anything. But it's not like you're telling him anything you shouldn't, and if you do find out there's something corrupt about this deal, you'll have the facts you need instead of just pissing off Gallagher."

"He's already pissed off."

"Well, instead of pissing him off more."

What Peter said made sense, but I couldn't help feeling uneasy. The very act of track-covering was an admission that I was fully aware what I was doing was wrong on some level, even if Gallagher's attitude left me with little choice.

By the time we got to sleep, it was after two, and it seemed as if the alarm went off only a moment later. It made me cranky that Peter got to roll over and go back to sleep, and it made me even crankier to have to take my things into the bathroom to get ready so I wouldn't wake him again.

The bathroom was a small room to start with, and for a man without much vanity, Peter had a lot of toiletries— toiletries that were taking up a disproportionate share of space in the shower and on the countertop. It had been handy to have him around the previous night, to have his help in figuring out how to respond to mysterious e-mails and hide the traces of my potentially criminal actions, not to mention the homemade meal, but there was nothing like accidentally taking a big slug of aftershave (the bottle of which bore a sly resemblance to my mouthwash) to bring home the practical realities of sharing an apartment in New York.

Given that he'd set the meeting time, Gallagher evidently didn't mind the hour; besides, his face was always haggard.

At least he'd actually shown up on time today. Jake looked like he'd just returned from a month of lounging on a Tahitian beach, and Mark was his usual bland self, but I was all too conscious of the dark hollows under my eyes and the bitter taste of aftershave in my mouth. We were in our same seats from the previous morning, and my hands had already assumed their tight grips on the armrests of my chair in anticipation of another dose of verbal abuse. Gallagher didn't disappoint.

"This is crap," he announced without preamble, tossing his copy of the materials we'd spent most of the previous afternoon and evening preparing into the trash. In obscenity-laden detail, he began enumerating the changes we'd need to make before the conference call he'd scheduled with Perry for later that day.

The buzz of the intercom interrupted him. He hit a button to put the phone on speaker. "Yeah?"

"It's your lawyer on line one," said Dahlia.

"Got it. And brew a fresh pot of coffee. The stuff you brought me tastes like crap." Gallagher hit another button on the phone. "Barry? How are the papers coming along?"

"We'll be ready to file in a couple of days," answered the disembodied voice.

"Let me know when the delivery's confirmed. Not that I won't hear from her the second she opens the envelope." The lawyer said something in response, and Gallagher said something back, and I settled in for another session of listening to Gallagher charmingly air his dirty laundry.

I managed to tune out most of the conversation, but

when he selected a pencil from the silver mug and rammed it into the sharpener, I couldn't block it out. Nor did I trust myself not to laugh if I caught Jake's eye after yesterday's discourse on "the pencil thing." Instead, I kept my gaze fixed stolidly ahead and tried to think about sad things, like abandoned puppies and global warming.

Sure enough, Gallagher inserted the newly sharpened end into his mouth and sucked on it, long and hard.

I dug my nails into my palms, trying to distract myself with the pain. Beside me, Jake made a weird noise that somehow combined a snort and a cough. Even Mark was pressing his lips together tightly, as if trying to ensure that no sound escaped.

Gallagher didn't seem to notice. He hung up a moment later and resumed his critique of our work as if there'd been no interruption.

"That's it," he said finally, after thoroughly ripping to shreds everything we'd done thus far. "I want to see another draft of everything by noon. Capiche?"

"Capiche," answered Jake.

"Okay, then," he said. "Get out of here." Hardly inspiring words, but anything that involved leaving his office sounded good to me.

We were almost out the door when he called us back. My earlier sense of déjà vu returned. At least today he wanted us all and not just me.

"There's one other thing."

He selected a fresh pencil from the mug, and we waited as he repeated his ritual with the sharpener. This time I had to work so hard not to react I worried that I might choke. Out of the corner of my eye, I could see Jake's shoulders shaking with suppressed laughter.

Thoughtfully, Gallagher lifted the pencil to his lips, and thoughtfully, he inserted the newly sharpened tip into his mouth as we waited for his final instructions.

But when he withdrew the pencil and opened his mouth to speak, all that emerged was a tortured gasp.

His eyeballs bulged, and a gurgle escaped from his throat, flecking his lips with blood-stained foam. His body jerked with spasms that pitched him out of his chair and onto the floor. His limbs flailed on the carpet as a horrifying wheezing sound came from his mouth.

I rushed to the door, to get help or tell someone to call an ambulance, but then the room went silent behind me.

Slowly, I turned around.

Gallagher lay still on his back, his eyes wide and unseeing. It was all over in a matter of seconds.

chapter nine

If we'd been doctors instead of MBAs, I suppose one of us would have tried CPR or something like that, but it seemed very clear that there was no bringing Gallagher back. A smell of burnt almonds tinged the air. I'd read about that scent in Agatha Christie books and had thought it was more a mystery novel convention than the real smell of cyanide. It turned out that she hadn't been making it up.

Jake crouched down by the dead man, checking awkwardly for a pulse. Mark stood frozen, motionless in the spot he'd been in when Gallagher took his fatal lick. We both watched as Jake rose slowly to his feet. He shook his head, a stunned expression on his handsome face.

Dahlia arrived on the scene just then. She took one look, dropped the coffee cup she'd been carrying, and then followed it to the floor in a faint. Rather than step over her to get to another phone, I reached over Gallagher's desk to call

911. Then I called Winslow, Brown security to explain that there was a dead banker on the 39th floor.

Paramedics arrived within minutes, followed closely by uniformed policemen, who were followed in turn by plain-clothes detectives. A photographer captured images of Gallagher's body sprawled on the carpet. Then a team from the medical examiner's office zipped up the corpse in a black rubber bag and wheeled it out, but not before the presumptive murder weapon had been extracted from the dead man's fingers and inserted into a labeled plastic envelope. My little joke about poisoning Gallagher by pencil no longer seemed so funny, although it had been surprisingly prescient.

Jake, Mark, Dahlia, and I were shepherded into separate conference rooms until we could each give the police a statement. By the time I reemerged, it was nearly noon, I'd spent way too much time on my own with nothing to do but think, and the authorities were clearing out. If it weren't for the yellow crime scene tape barring the door to Gallagher's office, you would hardly know that anything untoward had happened. Gallagher's death and the police presence were enough to generate a few hours' worth of buzz and gossip, but this was an investment bank, and there were deals to be done and money to be made—people were already busily at work, although there was an oddly hushed and sober feel to the floor.

I returned to my office in a daze. Jessica took one look at my face, followed me in, pulled a Diet Coke out of the refrigerator, and handed it to me without her usual lecture on how its various chemicals would rot those organs they weren't mummifying. She even opened it for me.

Peter wasn't at work when I called. "He had an appointment uptown," his assistant told me. I left a message for him and then tried his cell, but it went right into voice mail.

I was staring unseeingly at my computer screen when Jake came in.

"You okay?" he asked.

"No. I mean, yes. A bit freaked out, I guess." I'd seen dead people before, but I'd never actually watched anyone die. "How are you?"

He shrugged. "A bit freaked out, too. I rescheduled the call with Perry, by the way. He's a real piece of work. He seemed more concerned that this might slow down his deal than anything else."

I'd completely forgotten about the call, not to mention the laundry list of tasks Gallagher had assigned in his last minutes of life.

"Listen," Jake continued, "Mark, believe it or not, is already working on the revisions to the Thunderbolt materials. I don't think anyone would miss us if we skipped out of here for a bit. And I think we could both use a change of scenery."

It had been a long time since I'd found myself drinking during the middle of the day, much less in the middle of the work week, but when Jake said, "To hell with it" and ordered a bourbon on the rocks, I changed my Diet Coke to a glass of Pouilly-Fuissé.

We were a few blocks from the office in the Bar Room

of the 21 Club. The red-checked tablecloths and model air-planes and other trinkets hanging from the ceiling offered a cheery counterpoint to our less than cheery moods. We'd ordered food with our drinks, but neither of us could eat much. This was, for me at least, a clear indication that I really was freaked out. Our limited food intake, however, didn't stop us from proceeding on to a second and then a third round of drinks. Jake was sticking to the Maker's Mark, but I was alternating the wine with Diet Coke. Each beverage provided its own unique comfort.

"He wasn't the nicest guy," said Jake. "In fact, he was a total bastard. But nobody's ever died in front of me like that. And it looked so...*painful.*"

I grimaced. I didn't want to think about the convulsions, or the wheezing, or the strange cast to Gallagher's skin as he lay dead on his office floor, but the images and associated sound effects kept playing in my head and had a lot to do with my lack of appetite. "At least you didn't spend the last several days joking about how much you wanted him dead."

"You were only joking. Somebody else must have been a lot more serious."

"But who?" I asked. "I mean, it's one thing to think the guy's a schmuck or a bastard or whatever, it's another thing to poison his pencil." I couldn't get over how surreal and somewhat ludicrous death by poisoned pencil truly was. If anyone ever chose to murder me, I hoped they'd do it in a more dignified way. "Speaking of which, it had to be some-one who knew about the pencil thing."

"And had recent access to his pencil supply," Jake pointed out.

"Well, there's us," I said. "It wouldn't have been too hard for one of us to sneak a doctored pencil into the mug on his desk. It was just a plain old Number Two, nothing fancy. Is cyanide readily available?"

"What makes you say cyanide?"

I explained about the smell of burnt almonds and Agatha Christie.

"Interesting," he said. "I think cyanide's a common ingredient in a lot of pesticides, but I don't really know. Did you get a look at the pencil after the fact?"

"No. Why?"

"The entire tip was missing—I guess it came off in his mouth."

"Ugh." I pushed my plate of untouched food even farther away.

"Anyhow, we weren't the only ones in Gallagher's office lately. Dahlia's in and out of there constantly. And she's— she was probably in charge of his pencil supply."

"Dahlia? You can't be serious."

"Everybody said there was something going on between the two of them."

I shook my head. "I don't think so." I told him about my conversation with her in the ladies' room.

"So they weren't having an affair. But his treatment of her was pretty abusive. Maybe she just flipped?"

"You think she's seen *Nine to Five* one too many times?"

"Huh?"

"You know, *Nine to Five?* Dolly Parton, Jane Fonda, Lily Tomlin? They're all secretaries, and they have an evil boss, and they fantasize about how they'd kill him? And Lily Tomlin's character fantasizes about poisoning his coffee, and then she accidentally does?"

He was looking at me strangely. "*Forensic City,* Agatha Christie, and *Nine to Five?*"

"I have eclectic tastes." It seemed best not to mention the *Dawson's Creek* reruns.

"I'm beginning to see that."

"But I still can't picture Dahlia poisoning anyone."

"No, I have to admit, I can't, either."

"Then who did poison him?"

"Here's an idea," he said, rattling the ice in his glass. "Gallagher's daughter must be his primary heir—he wasn't the type to leave much to charity, and he probably made his current wife sign a pretty rigorous prenup. Naomi was in his office. If she'd been married to the guy, she must have known about the pencil thing, and she had the opportunity to slide a poisoned one into his mug when he wasn't looking. She'd probably be psyched for her daughter to come into her inheritance early."

I thought about that. "Well, if she did, it wasn't very smart of her to let half the department know that she would look so favorably on his dying. And when it comes to wives, his current wife was there, too. Annabel."

"What motive would she have?"

"Gallagher's money but no Gallagher. Sounds like a win-win to me."

"I bet he was worth more to her alive than he is dead."

"What do you mean?" I asked.

"I became friendly with my divorce lawyer when my wife and I were splitting up, and in the process I learned a bit about pre-nuptial agreements." He looked up with a rueful smile. "See—don't let anyone tell you that divorce doesn't have a silver lining—you get to meet new people and learn new things." He was striving for a light tone, but he was only partially successful.

"Good to know," I said, trying to match his tone, but I felt a pang of sympathy. Regular breakups were bad enough; I couldn't imagine how people got through a divorce. It made you wonder how people ever had the courage to get married in the first place.

"Anyhow, what Naomi said was probably right. Annabel will likely only end up with a share of whatever Gallagher made during the course of their marriage. Anything he made beforehand was probably excluded. That's how these things usually work. And they haven't been married for very long—just a couple of years."

"Gallagher must have made at least ten million just while they were married, though. That's nothing to sneeze at." Ten million was enough to buy a sufficiently large apartment that I'd never trip over Peter's boxes again. In fact, it was enough to buy each of Peter's boxes its own apartment.

"Not for most people. But a lot of it's probably already spent, and as for the remainder—let's just say, unless it was invested in something that really takes off, half isn't going to be enough to maintain the sort of lifestyle the second Mrs. Gallagher has been maintaining for very long."

"But were you listening to what Gallagher was saying this morning to his lawyer?"

"Hmm? No." Jake shook his head as he sipped his drink.

"About the papers being delivered, and how he was sure he'd hear from 'her' when they were? Maybe he was going to divorce her."

"In which case she'd end up with the same amount of money. Or maybe that's not what he was referring to at all. He could have just been trying to screw Wife Number One in some new way. Or maybe another 'she' entirely."

"Could be. He sure didn't seem like the faithful type."

"I still can't get over the way he came onto you," he said, shaking his head. "He really was a bastard."

"It happens."

"But in this day and age, and after all of the lawsuits you read about and diversity training and everything?"

"You'd be surprised." Maybe it was the wine on an empty stomach or maybe it was the shock of that morning—either way, I found myself telling Jake about some of the other uncomfortable encounters I'd had with male colleagues and my "insurance policy." It was nice to be able to talk to someone about it.

"It amazes me how sexist this profession still is," Jake said in disbelief. "It makes me ashamed to be a guy, practically. But it's a good idea, keeping a record like that."

"I just hope I'll never need it."

"Does anybody else know?"

"About the notebook? Just my friend, Luisa. It was her idea in the first place."

"Not even your fiancé?"

"Peter? No. He's already upset enough about how hard I work. And he gets angry when I tell him about partners acting like assholes; he'd go ballistic if he knew they were acting like lecherous assholes." I paused. "Why? Do you think I should tell him?"

Jake flashed his rueful smile again. "You're asking the wrong guy. As my ex-wife would attest, not to mention everyone I dated before her, I'm not exactly an expert at relationships." He took another sip of his bourbon.

"Me, neither." My track record before Peter had been more than a little checkered on the good judgment front. Then with a jolt I remembered the other thing I'd wanted to talk to Jake about. "I can't believe I forgot to tell you this," I said.

"Tell me what?"

"Last night. There was an anonymous e-mail on my home account about Perry and the Thunderbolt deal." I explained about the e-mail and what Peter and I had sent back.

"What a strange thing to happen."

"Mostly it was just creepy."

"I bet. I wonder why this Man of the People guy got in touch with you, specifically? How did he even know you were working on the deal? Do you think it's somebody who knows you but didn't want you to know who he is?"

"Could be. Although, I had another idea, too. Dahlia mentioned yesterday that two different people had called from Thunderbolt for a team list. Maybe one of them was actually this Man of the People guy and he was only pretending to be from Thunderbolt. She would have given out all of our names."

"Names, yes, but how did he get your personal e-mail address? And why did he contact you, instead of me? Or Mark, for that matter?"

Peter and I had discussed this at length. "He may have tried different variations of all of our names at all of the likely e-mail services—AOL, Hotmail, Verizon. My home account is nothing clever—just my first name and my last name plus my broadband provider. He could have sent out dozens of other e-mails, most of them to addresses that don't exist or belong to other people. And if they belonged to other people, they wouldn't have responded—they wouldn't have had any idea what the e-mail was about. And maybe he did try to e-mail you, and Mark, too, but he didn't hit on the right addresses?"

"I definitely didn't get anything on my Yahoo account. I checked it last night."

"I just hope I did the right thing. It felt wrong not to follow up in any way. If the deal is dirty, then it seems like I have a professional obligation to do something about it. But I didn't want to get anyone at the firm involved before I knew more, because I didn't want to give Gallagher even more reasons to hate me."

Jake nodded his head. "I think you did do the right thing. It was a bit of a catch-22, but you made the right decision.

Even with Gallagher out of the picture, it's probably better to find out what's going on before making any accusations."

"I'm glad you think so."

"Will you let me know if you hear back from this guy?" he asked. "We should definitely get to the bottom of this, especially since Perry's still so gung-ho on getting the deal done."

"Sure," I said.

It was good to know we were in this together.

chapter ten

We left 21 a little after three. I'd only had a glass and a half of wine when all was said and done, but I could definitely feel it as we walked back to the office. The bourbon seemed to have no effect whatsoever on Jake.

His cell phone rang on the walk back, and while nothing he said into it was particularly revealing, there was something about the way he spoke that made me think he was talking to a woman. An uncomfortable feeling washed over me. It took a moment to identify what, precisely, it was, and when I did, I wished I hadn't.

Jealousy.

This was inappropriate in every possible way, and I did my best to shunt it to the back of my mind, where it festered quietly for the rest of the day.

★ ★ ★

Four hours later I was sitting with another glass of white wine before me, but this time in the King Cole Bar at the St. Regis Hotel on East 55th Street. The rich colors of the Maxfield Parrish mural that gave the room its name glowed from the wall above the bar, tarnished somewhat from decades of cigar and cigarette smoke. Now the place was smoke-free, thanks to Mayor Bloomberg, and while the nicotine-deprived might complain, business was still going strong. Every table in the small lounge was full, and a throng of people occupied the remaining floor space, drinks in hand as they vied for the next empty table.

Fortunately, my friends had arrived before me and secured a cozy corner spot for us. It wasn't unusual for any of them to be in New York on occasion, but I couldn't remember the last time they'd all been here at once. Luisa had trained as a corporate lawyer and was even affiliated with a local law firm, but mostly she did work on behalf of her family in South America. Their international holdings were extensive and complex, and their affairs brought her here regularly. Emma, an artist, was a Manhattan native, but she'd been living in Boston with her boyfriend, Matthew, for the last few months. She was in New York to go over preparations for a gallery show that was going up in April. Hilary was a journalist, and she'd been camped out in Jane's guest room in Cambridge of late, putting the final touches on a true crime book about a string of serial killings that had occurred in the area. When she heard that Emma would be driving down, she hitched a ride and scheduled meetings with several publishers who'd shown interest. And when Jane heard that all of our other former roommates would be here at the same time, she'd arranged for a substitute at the school where she taught and insisted on coming along. "I'm nearly six months pregnant—this may be my last opportunity to go *anywhere* for a while," she explained.

"When's Peter getting here?" asked Emma.

"He's not," I said. "I thought it would be nice for it to be just us tonight." Peter had been concerned when we'd finally spoken by phone that afternoon. I had filled him in on what had happened that morning and the possibilities Jake and I had discussed. He urged me to pack it in early and head home, but I'd wanted to see my friends.

"How's the living-in-sin thing going?" asked Hilary, poking through the bowl of mixed nuts with her cocktail stirrer, searching for whichever kind she liked best.

"It's good," I said.

Jane, usually the most even-tempered among us, grabbed the bowl of nuts from Hilary. "Either take a nut, or don't take a nut," she snapped.

"How's the living-in-Jane's guest room thing going?" Luisa asked pointedly. Hilary scowled.

Jane turned to me. "I'm sorry, Rach. What were you saying?"

"Nothing. Just that living with Peter is good."

She raised an eyebrow. "Just good? Not wonderful? That's the word you usually use when it comes to Peter."

"No, it is wonderful. Really. He even cooked for me last night—lasagna."

"With what?" asked Emma. She'd spent a lot of time in my apartment.

"Apparently, I own a casserole dish." I took a sip of wine. "Anyhow, it's great to have him here. I think it's just going to take some time to get used to actually living together. The apartment's sort of small for two people, and there's definitely not enough closet space for two. I could barely fit my own stuff before. And Peter has his own stuff, and it's all over the place, and I don't know where we'll put everything. And I've been swamped at work, and I don't think he really realized before what my hours are like, much less the pressure of it all. And he doesn't seem to understand that sometimes I have to work late, and on weekends. And I gargled with his aftershave this morning, and it was really gross. And the whole thing is just sort of strange. To have someone there all of the time. It was never like that before."

As soon as all of these words spilled out of my mouth, I regretted them. I was lucky to have Peter, and I knew it, but I kept finding myself in the guilt/annoyance loop: first guilt for not loving every part of having him in my life, then annoyance about feeling guilty, and then a fresh wave of guilt at being annoyed.

"He lived in California before," Luisa reminded me. "And you only got to see him on weekends, after flying across a continent. I can't believe they don't let people smoke in bars in this fascist city." She was fidgety without her cigarettes.

"I know. It's much better this way than trying to sustain a relationship long-distance. Really. It's just that it's so...*permanent*."

"The last time I checked, you guys were getting married," Hilary said. "You might want to get a bit more comfortable with permanence."

"I am," I said, taking another fortifying sip of wine, "comfortable with it. It's what I've always wanted. Anyhow, ignore me. I'm babbling. It's just that it's been a really weird day."

"Why?" asked Emma.

"Somebody died in front of me. This morning, at work."

"Talk about burying the lead," said Hilary. "You're like *Hart to Hart*."

I stared at her. "I'm not following."

"Did you spend the eighties in a land with no TV? *Hart to Hart*. 'When they met, it was murder.' Only with you it's more like, 'Where she goes, there's murder.'"

The reference clicked in my mind. "Promise me you'll stage an intervention if Peter and I start driving matching Mercedes or get a dog named Freeway."

"A houseman might be sort of cool, even if he was named Max," said Jane.

"Besides, what makes you think it was murder?" I asked.

"Was it?" asked Emma.

"Well, yes. It seems to have been." I filled them in, rehashing the same material Jake and I had gone over that afternoon.

"What's the story with this Jake guy?" asked Hilary.

"Yes, his name is coming up quite a lot," added Luisa.

"He's just a friend from the office, and then he ended up working on the deal, too. He transferred in from Chicago a couple of months ago."

"Single?" asked Jane.

"Uh, divorced."

"What's he like?" asked Hilary.

"Standard-issue banker type."

"So, he's probably an utter jerk."

"No, not at all. He's a really good guy."

My friends exchanged not-so-subtle knowing looks with each other.

"What?" I asked.

"Somebody should do a case study on you," said Luisa.

"One of those relationship experts who writes self-help books about how to get men over their commitment issues," said Hilary. "Only it would be about getting women over their commitment issues. You could be an entire chapter."

"Just a chapter?" asked Luisa. "Rachel could fill more than a chapter."

"Now what are you talking about?" I asked.

"Your commitment issues," said Jane.

"I don't have commitment issues," I protested. I looked to Emma for backup.

"Sorry, Rach," she said. "You have commitment issues."

"Peter just moved in and instead of enjoying it you're whining about closet space and aftershave," said Hilary.

"I wasn't whining—"

"And every other word out of your mouth is the name of another man," said Luisa.

"Jake's just a friend—"

"A friend you spend more time with than you do your own fiancé," said Jane. "And who you tell things you avoid telling Peter."

"What are you scared of?" asked Emma.

"What do you mean, what am I scared of?"

"You must be scared of something," she said. "Why else would you be looking for reasons to shut Peter out?"

I wasn't sure how to respond to that, but it turned out I didn't have to because our waiter chose that moment to deliver a round of fresh drinks. His timing couldn't have been better as far as I was concerned. "Compliments of the gentlemen across the room," he said, depositing the glasses on the table.

"Oh?" Hilary craned her head to give our benefactors an appraising look. "Good Lord. What is it with men and goatees? They're so 1995. And they weren't even cool then."

"Could we tell them thanks but no thanks?" Emma asked. "And keep the drinks on our tab?"

"Why would we want to turn down free drinks?" asked Hilary.

"There's no such thing as a free drink. If we accept, they'll want to sit with us," said Luisa. The waiter left to deliver the message, but Hilary continued her inspection of the room.

"Of all the men here, only the goateed ones send us drinks. Why is that? I mean, check out the guy at the bar. How come guys like that never offer to buy us drinks?" she said. "In fact, I think he's checking you out, Rach. Why isn't he checking me out?"

I followed her gaze, catching a glimpse of a man with close-cropped dark hair across the room. He stood out in the sea of navy suits, dressed in faded jeans, an oxford-cloth shirt and suede jacket. For a fleeting instant our eyes met, but then he looked down at the beer he was nursing.

"I guess you're just a goatee magnet, Hil," said Jane.

"I know. It's a curse."

"Maybe you should stop fighting destiny," I suggested, relieved I was no longer the topic of discussion. But I was distracted, too. I'd seen the man before, and recently, but I couldn't remember where.

"It would probably feel nice and scratchy against your face," said Emma.

When I looked up again, a few minutes later, he was gone.

We went to a nearby restaurant for dinner after drinks. I was exhausted, but it was such a rare treat to have all of my friends in town that I lingered with them over the meal. We said our goodbyes on the pavement outside, making plans to get together later in the week. Jane was staying with Emma at the loft she still owned in the city, and Hilary was staying with Luisa at her family's apartment, so I was awarded the first cab since I was on my own.

I gave the driver my address on East 79th Street, and as he turned up Madison Avenue, I dug my BlackBerry out of my bag and used it to check messages, squinting at the small screen. There was only one voice mail, time-stamped 7:05 p.m., and I listened to it as we sped past Barney's.

"Rachel. It's Dahlia Crenshaw. Sorry to bother you, especially after the day we all had, but I was watching the news, and I saw something that—well, it got me wondering about something, and I wanted to talk to you about it. Will you phone me when you get this?"

She left her mobile number.

I dialed it in and pressed Send, but then I heard the beep of call waiting. I fumbled a bit with the various buttons. "Hold on," I said to whoever was calling as I tried to flip back to the call I'd placed.

"Dahlia?"

"Uh, no. It's Jake."

"Did I call you?" I asked, confused.

"No—I called you."

"Whoops, hold on." Jake must have been the incoming call. I pressed another few buttons but landed on Jake again. "Sorry about that," I said. "Still trying to master call waiting."

"No problem. Is it too late to phone?"

"No, of course not. You know I'm a night owl. What's up?"

"You seemed pretty shaken up today. I wanted to make sure you're doing all right."

"I am. Thank you. That's really kind of you to ask."

"Glad to hear it. And no more anonymous e-mails?"

"I don't know. I haven't checked that account yet. I'm actually in a cab right now, on my way home."

"And you thought I'd be Dahlia?"

I explained about her message. "I was just calling her back, and then you called."

"I wonder what she wanted?"

"She said it was about something she'd seen on the news. But maybe she just wanted to talk. Who knows? She must be pretty shaken up, too."

"Who could blame her? When did she call?"

"A while ago. Around seven." Then I checked my watch. It was after midnight, and she was probably long since in bed—it was a good thing my call hadn't gone through. "I'll catch up with her in the office tomorrow."

"I wouldn't worry about it. Anyhow, I'll let you go. Just wanted to make sure you were okay."

"Thanks, Jake."

The apartment was silent when I let myself in, and a quick peek into the bedroom showed me that Peter was fast asleep, although he'd left the lamp burning on the nightstand on my side of the bed. I returned to the study and waited impatiently as the computer booted up. My conversation with Jake had reminded me I needed to check the new e-mail account we'd set up the previous evening.

I entered my user name and password and waited expectantly for a message to appear. But Man of the People hadn't written back.

I felt both relieved and disappointed. It would have been nice to have some answers about the Thunderbolt deal. Gallagher's death had created enough intrigue for one day.

I undressed as quietly as I could and slid into bed beside Peter, careful not to wake him.

And all of my late nights and early mornings paid off for once, allowing me to drift quickly to sleep. Which was good, because the last thing I wanted to do was think.

chapter eleven

I overslept the next morning. Peter had turned off the alarm before it sounded.

"I made an executive decision," he told me. "You've been working too hard, and then you had to deal with this Gallagher guy dying at your feet. You deserved a decent night's rest."

It was a good thought, and he did bring a nice cold Diet Coke with him when he eventually woke me up at eight, but already running late so early in the day put me off-balance.

I managed to shower and get dressed without imbibing any of Peter's toiletries, although I knocked over his deodorant while drying my hair, which set off a domino-like tumbling of all of the products lined up on the counter next to it. It would have been fun to watch if I hadn't been in such a hurry.

Peter was on the phone in the living room when I emerged from the bedroom and crossed over into the study. I wanted to check e-mail again, to see if maybe Man of the People had written during the night, and it wouldn't do to log in from my work PC. I opened up the Web browser and selected "history" to get to the link for my new account. Without really looking, I selected the most recent listing, assuming that it would be the one I needed, since I thought I'd been the last one to use the computer. But instead of the page I expected, I found myself on the Winslow, Brown Web site, looking at Jake Channing's photo and professional biography.

That was odd.

I scanned the index of previous Web pages along the left-hand side of the browser more carefully and selected the second listing. This took me to a Google search on Jake Channing.

There was only one explanation for it, assuming I hadn't been Googling Jake in my sleep. And that was that Peter had been Googling Jake while I slept in.

"Peter?" I called out.

His head appeared in the doorway, the phone clasped to his ear. "That sounds like it meets the specifications," he was saying, presumably to whichever one of his company's engineers was on the other end. He held up an index finger to indicate he'd be done in a minute, and his head disappeared again. "And when do you think it could be ready? I see…" His voice trailed off into the living room.

I tried to think of reasons why Peter had been Googling

Jake, but I wasn't yet sufficiently caffeinated to come up with anything that made sense. Instead, I found the link to the new e-mail account and checked it. Still nothing. And Peter was still rambling on about specs and timetables.

Then I checked my regular home e-mail account, just in case. But while I had a whole slew of new e-mails from the Viagra folks, here, too, there was radio silence from Man of the People. And Peter was still on the phone.

I got out my BlackBerry to check messages at work, pressing Send without thinking. The number for my office voice mail was usually the last one I dialed every night, and when I pressed Send, the device automatically dialed the last number I'd used. So I was surprised when, instead of the familiar voice welcoming me to Audix, I heard Dahlia Crenshaw inviting me to leave a message.

Peter chose that moment to reappear in the study. "What can I do for you?" he asked. Startled, I hung up on Dahlia's recording.

"I was just wondering why you were Googling Jake Channing." It may have been a trick of the morning light, which was lending a rosy glow to the small room, but I could have sworn he blushed.

At least he didn't try to pretend he hadn't been doing any such thing. "I—I was curious. How did you find out? I thought I'd closed down the browser."

"You did. But I was using the history function. Why you were curious?"

"The history function? Why were you using that?"

"To get to the new e-mail account you set up for me. But I got to your Google search instead."

"Interesting. Did you—actually, never mind."

"I do mind. You haven't answered my question." It was a good thing I was still under-caffeinated, because with more stimulation, my voice would have sounded shrewish rather than just schoolmarmish.

"Which question?"

"Why were you curious about Jake Channing."

I was increasingly confident that it wasn't the light. Peter *was* blushing.

"Well, he called last night. Which was good, because I could check to make sure you wouldn't miss anything if I let you sleep in a bit."

"You Googled him because he called me?"

He hesitated. "It's just that then I scrolled through the caller ID and saw that he'd already called a couple of times, before I even got home."

"So?"

"Rachel. This is embarrassing."

"What's embarrassing?"

"Are you going to make me say this?"

"Say what?"

"Say that I was jealous."

"You were jealous?" I asked. "Jealous of what?" I probably should have been touched, or flattered. But instead I was angry.

"You keep mentioning him. And you're spending most of your waking hours with him."

"I *work* with him. We have a deal underway. I have to spend time with him."

"It's more than that, Rachel. Gallagher's dead and you're getting strange e-mails. And now that you've told Jake about Man of the People—I just wanted to make sure that you can trust him. So I thought I'd do a little research."

"I can trust him," I said.

"Did you know that he worked at Gallagher's old firm?" Peter asked. "Did he tell you that?"

"Of course I knew."

"And you don't think there's a chance he could be in on any of this? You think it's just a coincidence?"

"You're being absurd. Jake joined Winslow, Brown way before Gallagher came over from Ryan Brothers. And if Jake was in on anything with Gallagher—and by the way, we still don't know if there's anything to be in on in the first place—Gallagher sure had a strange way of showing it. He was nearly as much of a jerk to him as he was to m—to anyone."

"Maybe. But I'm worried that you're not being as careful as you should be. That you're letting your feelings get in the way."

"What feelings?"

"Are you going to make me say this, too?"

I looked at him but didn't say anything. There was a long moment of silence.

Then he turned away from me. "Your feelings for Jake," he said.

Something inside of me switched off and something else

switched on. It was as if I'd been waiting for a reason—any reason—to blow up at Peter, and he'd just handed it to me. When I spoke again, I felt like I was on autopilot or having an out-of-body experience. On some level I fully recognized that I was lashing out at the wrong person, but I couldn't help it.

"Jake is my colleague and my friend, Peter. Nothing more." My autopilot voice was cold. I stood up and began gathering my things. "And I can take care of myself. I've been doing it for a long time. Since before I met you and since before you moved in."

"Rachel, I was—I am concerned. I'm only trying to help."

"By accusing me of being involved with other men?"

"I wasn't accusing you of being involved—"

"And completely invading my privacy?"

He took a step back. "How was I invading your privacy?"

"Investigating my colleagues. Spying on my caller ID."

"*Spying* on *your* caller ID?"

"What would you call it?"

"First of all, I couldn't help but see the caller ID when I went to use the phone. And second of all, it happens to be my caller ID, too."

"How is it your caller ID?"

"I live here. Remember?"

"How can I forget?"

"What's that supposed to mean?" he asked, following me as I crossed the living room.

"It means I gargled with your aftershave yesterday. Your stuff is everywhere."

"That's because you don't have a spare second to help me figure out where I can put everything."

"I've been working," I said, shoving my arms into my coat sleeves.

"It's not just about finding a place for my stuff, Rachel, or about giving me a set of keys."

"Now, what's *that* supposed to mean?"

"It means that it's about finding a place for *me*." He took a deep breath. "Do you even want me here? And I don't just mean in this apartment or in this city."

"Are you saying you don't want to be here?"

"No—"

"You want things to go back to the way they were?"

"No—"

I tore his ring off my finger and threw it down on the hall table. "Because that can be arranged, Peter."

"Rachel—"

"And now I'm really behind schedule. We'll have to talk about this later."

He caught my arm. "Rachel," he said again.

I pulled my arm away. "I don't have time for this. We'll talk about it later," I repeated.

And then I slammed the door.

chapter twelve

I was off autopilot and completely appalled with myself by the time I hit the street.

My friends had been right. I was scared. The fear was so tangible I could practically taste it. And it was safer to feel angry than to feel vulnerable.

So I'd just picked a fight—a really big, potentially irreparable, and wholly unjustified fight—with my fiancé. I'd been horrible to him, all because our relationship and everything that came with it terrified me. Something inside me seemed determined to torpedo the entire thing, to preserve my single but stable independence rather than take the risk that things with Peter might not work out.

And unless I figured out a way to stop being scared, any attempt to patch things up with Peter would be nothing more than a temporary fix.

But I didn't know how to stop being scared. And I definitely didn't have time for extended psychotherapy, however much I might need it.

So I did what I usually did when I didn't want to deal
with uncomfortable emotions: I turned my thoughts to
work and the day ahead. This would probably be hard for
most people to do in a similar situation, but I'd had a lot of
practice being dysfunctional.

There was no good way to get to the office when I left
this late. The subway would be a crowded nightmare, it was
still too cold and slushy to go by foot, and the odds of finding a taxi in my neighborhood at this time of the morning
were pretty much nil. I spent the two-block walk to the subway entrance at 77th Street and Lexington scanning the
streets for an unoccupied cab. But when one didn't appear,
I descended reluctantly down to the turnstiles for the 6 train.

I just missed a train leaving the station, which could only
be expected given how my day was going so far. I joined
the other commuters on the platform to wait for the next
train to arrive. While people were generally relatively civ-
ilized on the subway, there seemed to be something in the
air today, an unusual tension as people jockeyed for position.
Rush hour always made me nervous—you had to be careful that an inadvertent shove didn't send you flying into the
path of an oncoming train. I just hoped nobody shoved me,
because I didn't trust myself not to shove back on this particular morning.

I should have called in sick, I thought to myself. I never

did, even when I actually was sick. I'd earned more than an extra hour's sleep—I'd earned a good sick day, what with never calling in sick and working late and on weekends and then having to watch people die hideous pencil-induced deaths. I briefly fantasized about going home, changing into pajamas, and catching up on my TiVo backlog. Of course, all of this assumed that the wreckage of a relationship wouldn't be waiting for me in the apartment. I stayed where I was.

Ten minutes elapsed before the next train pulled in, and while it looked packed to capacity, the crowd at my back propelled me through the doors. I found myself in the middle of the car, unable to reach a pole or overhead grip, but it didn't matter, as the people smushed up against me made it impossible to move in any direction, much less lose my balance. I shut my eyes—I didn't want to be able to identify what might be pressing into me from every side.

It took only five or six minutes to get to the 51st Street stop, but it took me nearly as long again to emerge from the station, which served not only the 6 train but other lines from the various New York boroughs. By the disgruntled looks on the faces I passed and the Metropolitan Transit officials hurrying about, funneling people along, I guessed that maybe one of the lines was out of service, further exacerbating the everyday gridlock of the morning commute. Up on the street, I trudged the remaining blocks to my office, skirting piles of soot-darkened snow and murky puddles as best I could and wondering again why I hadn't called in sick.

A half hour later, I was really wishing I had.

★ ★ ★

The floor was strangely deserted when I arrived. I checked my watch—it was well after nine, and the place should be humming with activity. Instead it was eerily quiet.

I started toward my office, but then I saw that all of the people who weren't out on the floor were gathered in one of the glass-walled conference rooms. Had somebody called an impromptu staff meeting? Perhaps to discuss Gallagher's murder? Why was it that the one day in the last year when I wasn't the first to arrive in the office would be the one day that the partners decided it was time for an impromptu all-department chat?

But when I got to the conference room, the first thing I noticed was that none of the partners seemed to be there—in fact, it was mostly support staff and a handful of junior bankers. Since many of the partners did the bulk of their work while golfing in Palm Beach, skiing in Aspen, or steaming at the University Club, it was not unusual for our floor to be a partner-free zone in the mornings. At least their absence assured me I hadn't missed an important meeting.

The second thing I noticed was that everyone's attention was focused on the TV, which was tuned to New York 1, the local news cable channel.

"What's going on?" I whispered to the guy on my left, rising on tiptoe to get a better look at the screen. He shushed me. He must have been new, because I didn't know his name, but I glared at him—I was in no mood to be shushed—and turned my attention back to the TV.

A perky-looking reporter was holding forth, attempting

gravitas. "—just a few minutes ago, at the scene of this shocking crime."

"What crime?" I asked the guy on the other side of me. I didn't know his name, either, but he wore the navy polo shirt and khakis that were the standard uniform of Winslow, Brown's mail-room clerks.

"The dead dude's assistant."

"Dahlia?"

"Yeah. You know, the one with the—"

The guy on my left shushed us both, which was probably a good thing, given where the guy on my right seemed to be going and my likely reaction.

The camera switched from the perky reporter to a shot of her surroundings. "—Below Citicorp Center," she was saying. I realized she was standing in front of the entrance to the subway station I'd just come from.

"Oh my God," I said. "I was just there." The guy on my left shushed me again, and I ignored him. "What happened?" I asked the other guy.

"Somebody pushed her in front of a subway car. But it didn't run her over. It stopped in time."

"Is she all right? And how do we know it's her? Dahlia, I mean?"

"They found her Winslow, Brown security pass and called. And they're not saying if she's all right."

"That's why we're trying to listen to the TV, here," the guy on my left pointed out.

"Oh."

The reporter was now interviewing a commuter, a witness, I guessed. Her microphone was pointed at his face, and he was speaking into it excitedly. "Like, I was waiting for the train, you know? And this one woman was talking to this other woman, and like I wasn't paying attention, you know?"

The reporter started to give a perky nod, but remembering that she was supposed to be serious, raised her eyebrows instead.

"Anyhow," the man continued, "The train was coming, and the next thing I know, it's like everybody's screaming, you know, and I guess the one woman fell onto the tracks, and then the other woman, she like ran past me? And somebody was yelling, 'She pushed her, she pushed her?'"

"Can you describe this other woman? The alleged pusher?" I could tell that the reporter liked using the word "alleged."

"She was pretty normal looking. Like, medium size and everything."

"Did she have any distinguishing characteristics?" The reporter seemed to like saying "distinguishing characteristics," too. "Unusual features or items of clothing that you noticed?"

"She had, like, long red hair? Sort of curly? And, like, a bright green hat and scarf?"

A silence fell over the room.

I turned toward the door, wondering if someone new had come in and if that was the reason for the sudden quiet.

Then I realized everyone was looking at me.

Or, more precisely, at my hair, which was long and red and sort of curly, and at the tail end of my scarf, which was trailing harmlessly from my shoulder bag.

It was bright green.

chapter thirteen

The silence continued, unbroken except by the perky reporter, who was summarizing what the witness had told her for the benefit of those just tuning in. But nobody seemed to be paying attention anymore.

My face felt stiff, as if my smile muscles had been injected with Botox. "Well, I guess I'll be getting to work now."

The whispering started as soon as I turned my back.

I sat in my office with the door closed, a Diet Coke gripped tightly in one hand and my browser open to the New York 1 Web site, which offered an online audio feed of its live broadcast. The reporter didn't have much new information, so she kept repeating what she already knew: Dahlia had been pushed onto the subway tracks and narrowly avoided being run over by an oncoming car that had screeched to a stop mere inches away, and her unidentified assailant, who was apparently a mirror image of me, had managed to escape in the ensuing chaos. Dahlia herself had been rushed to a hospital, unconscious.

I muted the sound from my PC and started to call Peter. The shock of the news had wiped the morning's earlier events from my mind. But then it all came flooding back.

I definitely couldn't call him unless I was ready to apologize, and I wouldn't even know where to begin. No simple "I'm sorry" would suffice after everything I'd said. And I wasn't even sure it would be fair to apologize, because it wasn't in Peter's best interests to forgive me. It was one thing for me to be completely screwed up inside my head, but it was inexcusable to take the screwiness out of my head and dump it on Peter. I was an emotional menace, and potentially a danger to society.

I thought about calling one of my friends, but it would be impossible to explain everything that had happened that morning over the phone, and I wasn't sure if I could handle the inevitable lecture that was likely to follow, even if it was justified.

My next thought was to call Jake, but as soon as I started to dial, I could hear the hurt in Peter's voice as he suggested I had feelings for him, and that my feelings were getting in the way of my judgment.

I put the phone down before I could finish dialing. I still hadn't untangled the knot of emotions that had caused me to flip out at Peter, but it seemed like now would be a good time to figure out what, precisely, I felt for Jake before I tangled the knot further.

I couldn't deny the flash of jealousy yesterday. Or the warmth in my cheeks at lunch on Monday.

But there'd also been Jake's welcome support in a work environment that had been more than a little stressful of late. He'd helped me deal with Gallagher's pass and all of the hostility that came after it, not to mention his ugly death. And he'd done it all with understanding and discretion. I'd trusted him with a lot, and he hadn't disappointed that trust.

Maybe I did have a small crush—but it was harmless, the sort of thing that was bound to happen when you worked closely with someone who was interesting and attractive. It didn't mean anything, really, and it didn't change the fact that Jake had been nothing but kind from the moment we met. He was my friend, and I hoped he considered me his friend, too. He must, I thought, remembering his self-deprecating comments about his failed marriage—that wasn't the sort of thing you shared with just anybody.

And just because I'd gone looking for trouble in my relationship with Peter didn't mean I should go looking for trouble in every other relationship I had.

I picked up the phone again and dialed his extension but his assistant answered. "He's on the other line," she told me. "I'll have him get back to you." I probably was being paranoid, but I thought I could detect an iciness in her tone that had never been there before.

Frustrated, I tried to come up with someone else to call, but I was fresh out of names. Desperate for distraction, I began scrolling through my e-mails and even flipped through the new analyses Mark Anders had dropped off for the Thunderbolt deal, but I couldn't absorb a single word or number.

Ten minutes later, Jake hadn't returned my call and New York 1 had moved on to other topics. Meanwhile, my office walls felt as if they were closing in on me, and while the members of the department hadn't yet grouped outside my door with pitchforks and torches, I suspected that plans to do so were afoot somewhere on the floor.

I could use some fresh air, I decided. I pulled my hat and scarf out of my bag and shoved them under the desk. "I'll be back in a bit," I told Jessica.

For a variety of reasons that seemed, in retrospect, not terribly well-reasoned, I had determined by my senior year of college that I wanted to pursue a career in investment banking. Most of the major investment banks recruited on campus, and I submitted my résumé to them all. Probably nobody was more surprised than I when several of them extended job offers.

My decision came down to Winslow, Brown and two other firms. All three were considered top-tier Wall Street institutions, but the other two took the entire "Wall Street" thing a bit too seriously. Their offices were actually located downtown, in Manhattan's financial district. Winslow, Brown's midtown headquarters, on the other hand, were around the corner from Saks Fifth Avenue and only minutes from the time-honored trifecta of Bendel's, Bergdorf's, and Barney's.

The decision was an easy one, and the choice I'd made to return to Winslow, Brown after business school had been based on similar criteria.

I was back to operating on autopilot as I left the office, my thoughts consumed with questions about who my unknown twin was, why she would want Dahlia dead, and what the connection could be, if any, with Gallagher's murder. My feet, either out of habit or because they had a better understanding of what was happening than my brain did, delivered me to the side entrance of Saks on East 50th Street.

I didn't actually try anything on, but browsing through the designer collections occupied the better part of an hour, and the contemporary collections on the fifth floor took up the remaining part. My thoughts still weren't very clear when I rode the escalators down to the ground floor and the accessories counters, but on some level I was already aware that it wouldn't do to use a credit card and leave a digital trail of my whereabouts and purchases. Fortunately, I'd gone to the ATM a few days before and my wallet was stuffed with bills. I parted with some of them to pay for a pair of oversize black sunglasses, and I parted with some more to buy a black wool hat with a big, floppy brim.

I took the escalators back up a few flights and went into the ladies' room. It was empty—Wednesday mornings in March tend not to be prime shopping time for most Manhattan retailers, and tourists were more likely to hit Bloomingdale's or Macy's than Saks. There was an elastic band in my handbag, which I used to anchor my long, curly red hair in a makeshift chignon. I liberated my new hat from its tissue wrappings and removed the store tags before placing it on my head. Then I slipped my new sunglasses over my face.

The reflection in the mirror was practically unrecognizable. But if I'd been thirty pounds lighter, several inches shorter, and clutching a Starbucks cup, I might be in danger of being mistaken for an Olsen twin.

The sun was shining brightly when I emerged from the store, so I didn't even need to feel self-conscious about my wraparound shades, and it was fun to be able to stare at everyone around me without them even knowing I was staring. My office and the assorted responsibilities waiting for me there were beginning to exert their usual gravitational pull, but I wasn't ready to go back to work, much less deal with the unresolved mess I'd made of my personal life. I crossed Fifth Avenue, thinking I'd do a bit more window-shopping.

There was a buzzing in my handbag, but I ignored it the first time. Unfortunately, it buzzed again a few minutes later, and then again a few minutes after that. The third time I grimaced and dug out my BlackBerry. I had a number of new messages, as the buzzing had indicated. One of the nicest things about Saks was that the cellular reception was lousy, so it was a good place to go if you didn't want anyone calling you. At least, calling and actually getting through. But once I got outside, in clearer range of the closest cellular transmitter, all of the messages flooded in.

I scanned the list of missed calls. A couple bore the telltale number of the Winslow, Brown switchboard, a couple

I didn't recognize, and the last one had been dialed from my apartment. I was debating whether or not I actually wanted to listen to any of the messages when the phone rang. Once again, the number on the screen was that of my apartment.

Peter, I guessed. It would be just like him to call to apologize when I was the one who owed him an apology.

"Hi," I said, trying to figure out what to say next. Maybe I could tell him that I was working on my apology and would get back in touch when it was ready?

"Fred," he said. "Glad I caught you. It's Peter Forrest."

"It's not Fred, it's Rachel," I said. "Who's Fred?"

He chuckled, which was weird. Peter wasn't a chuckler. "Listen, Fred. I've had an unexpected visit this morning, and I'm going to have to reschedule our meeting."

I may have owed Peter an apology, and I may have been an emotional menace, but that didn't mean I was in any mood for games. "Peter, what's going on? This isn't Fred. You know damn well who you called."

"It's funny, Fred—one of the guys reminds me of that O'Connell chap, from Boston. Or maybe more of that O'Donnell character we met last summer?"

Not only was Peter not a chuckler, I'd never heard him refer to anyone as either a "chap" or a "character" before. "Okay, now this is just stupid—"

Then I realized what Peter was doing. The two of us knew only a couple of police officers personally. One was a Detective O'Connell in Boston, whom I'd helped—more by accident than on purpose—to track down a serial killer a couple of months ago. The other was a Detective

O'Donnell, who worked in a small town in the Adirondacks where I'd had the misfortune to discover the body of Emma's former fiancé back in August. I leaned against a shop window and brought the phone closer to my mouth, using a hand to shield my words from the ears of passers-by.

"The police are in the apartment?" I asked.

"Sure, Fred. Your offices are pretty busy, too."

"And they were looking for me at work?"

"That sounds great."

"And you're trying to warn me."

"Right, right."

"I'm a suspect? They think I killed Gallagher?"

"It could be even more than that," he agreed, his voice still unnaturally jolly.

"And Dahlia? They think I tried to kill Dahlia?" It was hard to keep my own voice down given the wave of panic that was washing over me.

"Those projections seem to be on target. Listen, Fred, I have to go, but I'll have someone get in touch with your team to reschedule."

"My team?"

"What's that, Fred? This isn't the right number to use?"

"You're saying that I shouldn't call you. Because you think they'll be tracing the calls you get?"

"Right back at you, Fred. Take care, now."

"Wait—"

There was a click, and then he was gone.

chapter fourteen

I was having a bit of a head-spinning moment. Suddenly, it seemed as if everyone on the street was staring at me, as if my sunglasses no longer offered a protective shield and the eyes around me could penetrate their dark lenses and see through to the murder suspect lurking behind.

The crowded avenue and the brightly lit shops felt newly perilous, and I needed to sit down, preferably somewhere quiet and safe, in order to get the head-spinning under control. Fortunately, a quick scan of my surroundings presented a handy interim solution.

It was relatively easy to lose myself in the stream of tourists pouring into St. Patrick's Cathedral. Given that I'd never been inside the church before, I probably should have tagged along with one of the groups, listening to what a guide had to say, but I was in no condition to fully appreciate the building's architectural, artistic, and various other fine points. Instead, I took a seat in a pew about a third of the way down the nave and tried not to hyperventilate.

After a few minutes of determined deep breathing, I didn't feel fully composed, but I was collected enough to take an initial inventory of the situation.

Glenn Gallagher had been murdered, and I was a suspect in his murder. I knew this was preposterous, but it wasn't completely unreasonable that the police might see things differently. I'd definitely spent a lot of time telling people how happy I'd be to see Gallagher dead—in fact, I'd even joked about poisoning his stupid pencils, although I doubted that Jake or Mark had bothered to tell anyone about that. Still, I had a well-documented motive of sorts. While I knew I hadn't really meant it—I'd just wanted the guy out of my life—surely the authorities were duty-bound to investigate anyone who'd been saying anything that could be construed as a threat. I'd had plenty of time to slip doctored pencils into the mug on Gallagher's desk, so I had the opportunity, as well. As for means—cyanide couldn't be that hard to come by, and while I wouldn't have the foggiest idea as how to get the cyanide into the pencil, the actual murderer had figured it out, so it couldn't be that much of a challenge.

But this all seemed too flimsy to result in the police taking the trouble to hunt me down at home when they couldn't find me at work.

Which meant that they were likely there because of Dahlia instead of or in addition to Gallagher, as Peter had indicated. They had the unfortunate eyewitness testimony that somebody matching my description had pushed her onto the subway tracks, and there was probably footage from surveillance cameras, as well. And I'd paid for my MetroCard with a credit card, so perhaps they could even track when and where I'd gone through the subway turnstiles. I did some quick calculations—the timing would have been tight, but if I'd caught the train I'd just missed—I could have been at the 51st Street station at the right moment. I hadn't, of course, but would anybody do the work to try and find witnesses or video placing me where I actually was when they already thought they knew? And what they thought they knew seemed to be sufficient that Peter, who under normal circumstances would be the first to suggest that I turn myself in and get things straightened out in a reasonable manner, was suggesting that it would be best to make myself scarce.

I wondered if I was missing anything. I replayed the conversation with Peter in my head, trying to glean what little information I could from his cryptic words. Was there a reason he called me Fred, for example? I didn't know any Freds, and he'd never mentioned any to me, but was it a code of some sort? I played with the letters, rearranging them, but neither Derf, Dref, Erdf nor any of the other possible combinations meant anything to me.

Then my BlackBerry buzzed, reminding me again that I had messages waiting. And I remembered Peter's warning about his calls being traced, and his "right back at you" response. The entire conversation had been awkward, but this comment had struck me as particularly awkward. Could he have meant that calls to and from me could be traced, too?

That, in contrast to the answers I was getting from playing with the letters in Fred, actually made sense. Dahlia had called this number the previous evening, and I'd called her back. I hadn't managed to speak to her, but there were probably records of the calls in the computers of my wireless carrier.

And then I remembered that last night wasn't the only time I'd called her. I'd called her this morning, too, by accident when I thought I was calling my office voice mail—less than half an hour before she was pushed off the subway platform. Some people might find that incriminating, especially if they were already disposed to incriminate me.

I wondered how it could be possible for the police to get the phone records so quickly. On TV, they usually had to get a subpoena or something like that, approved by a judge.

But then I realized that they didn't need access to phone records. All they needed was Dahlia's cell phone, which she'd undoubtedly had with her when she was attacked, and its log of incoming and outgoing calls.

My impersonator may have taken the trouble to make it look like I'd tried to kill Dahlia, but I'd unwittingly come to her aid, using the device to construct a web of supporting evidence.

Then I remembered a movie I'd seen, in which the good guys tracked down a bad guy by the cell phone he had on him, triangulating his location based on the signals the phone was transmitting to and from different cellular towers.

Could somebody be triangulating my own location in the same way, closing in on me, even as I sat here?

It seemed unlikely that that sort of manhunt—personhunt—could already be underway, but if I was indeed a suspect, and if they thought I'd attempted murder twice in twenty-four hours, even if I'd only succeeded once—for all they knew, I was on some sort of crazed killing spree and had to be stopped.

I pulled the BlackBerry out of my bag and stared at it in horror.

I quickly powered off the device, but it still made me nervous. Perhaps it could continue to transmit information about my whereabouts even without power.

I thought about leaving it in the church, under the seat or in a confessional or something, but that seemed like it would only hasten its discovery and the associated discovery that I wasn't with it. And I needed to find another safe haven, too, because even if they didn't find my phone here, the data would in some way show that I'd been in this spot. At least that's how it had worked in the movie. I wondered how fugitives who didn't enjoy popular culture ever managed to remain at large.

Finding a place for the phone turned out not to be so hard. An open side pocket beckoned from the backpack on the back of the tourist in front of me in the line leaving the cathedral, and I slipped the BlackBerry in unnoticed. With any luck, if it was still emitting a signal, and if that signal was indeed being tracked, it would lead its followers to Omaha or some place like that, by way of a matinee of *The Lion*

King, a carriage ride through Central Park, and a Circle Line cruise.

But I still needed to find a place where I could sit quietly, undisturbed and with little chance of apprehension while I figured out what I was going to do next. Thinking about the Circle Line had planted the seed of an idea, and when I saw one of those red double-decker buses lumbering across Fifth Avenue, it seemed like fate was trying to tell me something.

Not only had I never been to St. Patrick's before, I'd never taken a Gray Line tour of the city, even though the buses regularly passed in front of my office building, ferrying tourists from midtown to United Nations Plaza on the East River. Nobody would ever think to look for me on a tour, and I liked the idea of staying on the move without actually having to move.

I strode through Rockefeller Center at a brisk but, I hoped, inconspicuous pace. The attendant in the box office at Radio City Music Hall sold me a ticket without even looking up from the paperback he was reading, but I still kept my sunglasses on as I made my purchase. A bus pulled up a few minutes after I pocketed the change.

Given the chill to the air, most of the passengers had opted for the enclosed lower deck. I had my new hat to keep me warm, and I preferred privacy, so I took the stairs to the upper deck, doing my best not to look furtive as I went. I had a wide selection of seats from which to choose.

I slid down an empty row and set about formulating a plan.

chapter fifteen

It was dark by the time I climbed up to the pedestrian walk-way over Hudson Street. I could smell the exhaust from the commuters' cars below, their engines idling as traffic moved slowly through the Holland Tunnel and into New Jersey.

Concrete stairs led down to the cobblestones of Laight Street and its string of converted warehouses and factories. I ventured along the sidewalk with careful steps, alert to any danger that might be lurking in the shadows.

But I reached the familiar door without encountering any lurking dangers. With a sigh of relief I pressed the button for the fifth floor.

"Yes?" The voice over the intercom was wary.

"It's me."

Caution gave way to impatience. "It's about time." The buzzer buzzed and I pushed the door open.

The hike up the four steep flights of stairs actually felt good after the several hours I'd spent on the bus. Its route had looped through midtown, over to the U.N. and then down to the South Street Seaport and the office towers of Wall Street before heading back up to Times Square and midtown. The narrative that came over the speakers had been interesting at the beginning, but it grew dull with repetition—even the same jokes were repeated. Fortunately, I felt I had enough of a plan to disembark in Tribeca before the bus headed uptown for the third time.

The first part of my plan involved finding a hideout that was warm, comfortable, and equipped with Diet Coke and other important staples. In addition to meeting these criteria, Emma's loft would be a relatively safe retreat given its out-of-the-way location and that it lacked the potentially prying eyes of a doorman. It had the further advantage of being accessible, because if Emma turned out not to be home, I had a convenient copy of her key stashed on my key ring. And if she were home, I doubted that she would turn me in to the cops.

Instead, when I finally emerged from the stairwell, she was standing in the open doorway holding out a glass of white wine.

"We thought you'd never get here. Are you hungry? We were thinking of ordering Thai."

My friends had been awaiting my arrival since midafternoon. They'd anticipated the thought process that would lead me to Emma's loft—in fact, they'd arrived at my decision well before I had. They probably hadn't wasted as much time trying not to hyperventilate and getting rid of spy phones.

"How's our favorite fugitive from justice?" Jane said by way of greeting.

"Assuming there's actually a warrant out for Rachel's arrest, which is probably premature, let's remember that technically neither Rachel nor anybody here knows she's a fugitive from justice," warned Luisa. "Otherwise, we'd be harboring a fugitive. And this isn't my area of expertise, but I'm fairly confident that would be against the law."

"So you've heard the whole story?" I asked.

"Matthew called me," Emma explained. "Peter called him from a pay phone, apparently being very cloak-and-daggers about the whole thing. He was concerned enough about his call being traced, even from the pay phone, that he didn't want it to go to any of our cell phones or homes. I guess he thought Matthew's clinic was the best option—he even dialed the switchboard rather than Matthew's direct extension as an extra precaution. If anyone were actually tracing the call, it would probably take awhile to figure out that Matthew was the person he called and that his girlfriend was your college roommate."

At least I wasn't the only one being paranoid about phones. I'd been scared to even use a pay phone. Not that there was one on the bus.

"And then Matthew called Emma, and Emma called us," said Luisa. "We figured you'd come either to my apartment or here, but since my building has a doorman, we thought you'd choose here." Luisa's family practically owned a small South American country, and their New York apartment had more than a doorman—it had a staff that included a butler, a cook, and assorted other uniformed attendants. It was a great place to hang out if you wanted your every whim catered to, but it probably wasn't the place to be if you wanted to minimize personal interactions.

"We've been waiting for you," said Jane. "But we thought you'd be here sooner—we were starting to worry."

"And for Peter to get so worked up, when he's usually so calm—we knew that whatever was happening had to be serious," added Emma.

"Little did we know that you'd cooked up such a clever disguise, Rach. It's a good look on you. Is it Mary-Kate or Ashley that you're going for?" asked Hilary.

In addition to the warmth, comfort and availability of certain caffeinated beverages, I'd chosen Emma's apartment because I knew it was the most likely to yield another important part of my plan. If the police thought I'd killed Gallagher and attempted to kill Dahlia, they would be focusing all of their efforts on finding me and further building their case against me.

Which meant that nobody was trying to find out who the real murderer was. And not only was unmasking the killer a prerequisite for clearing my name and returning to business as usual, it seemed to be the only way to guarantee that he or she—and a lot of what I knew implied that it could very well be a she—wouldn't strike again.

However, tracking down a killer wasn't going to be easy when I was a fugitive. I needed help.

There was Peter, of course. But even if I hadn't been so awful to him, and even if I had been able to deliver a decent apology, it wasn't possible to turn to him in this situation, when the police were probably tracking his movements and communications in the hope that he'd lead them to me.

No, I knew who I needed, and that unusual twist of events that had brought all of my friends to the city this week now seemed especially fortuitous. And, fortuitously, they all seemed eager to come to my aid. In fact, they were surprised that I bothered to ask.

"Why do you think we've spent the entire afternoon cooped up here, waiting for you to show?" Hilary replied.

Emma called in an order to a restaurant around the corner. "I'll pick it up instead of having them deliver," she said. "That way we don't have to worry about a deliveryman seeing you, and I can stop at a pay phone and call Matthew. Then he can call Peter and let him know you're safe." She giggled. "We'll have to figure out a code. Like 'the eagle has landed' or 'full moon over Tulsa' or something like that. Rachel, is there any special message you want to get to him?"

I opened my mouth, but I wasn't sure what to say. Asking Emma to tell Matthew to tell Peter I was sorry could hardly undo the damage I'd wrought. As apologies went, that would be setting a whole new standard for lame.

"Rachel?"

"We're sort of in a fight," I confessed sheepishly.

"Excuse me?" asked Jane.

"What could you possibly fight about with Mr. Too-Good-To-Be-True?" asked Hilary.

"You're being ridiculous about something, aren't you?" asked Luisa.

"Yes," I admitted. "It's pretty much all my fault."

And everything that had happened that morning came spilling out.

"So," summarized Hilary when I'd finished, "You're never home, but you have plenty of time to flounce around with some guy from work. And meanwhile, Peter's moved three thousand miles to do nothing but be supportive and sweet and cook for you and hack e-mail accounts for you and bring you Diet Coke in bed, and you pick a fight and accuse him of espionage?"

I would be the first to say my behavior had been deplorable, but it all sounded even worse when she put it like that.

"Why are you trying to drive him away?" asked Jane.

"Because you were right. I'm scared."

"Of what?" asked Emma.

"I don't know, exactly. I mean, there are all the usual clichéd answers: I'm scared of losing my independence, and I'm scared of things not working out. But none of that excuses taking it out on Peter. Is it even fair to ask him to forgive me? Wouldn't he be better off getting rid of me and finding some nice emotionally stable person to marry?"

"You're completely insane," said Hilary.

"That's exactly my point," I said.

My friends were eager to settle in for a long session of psychoanalysis with me as their subject, but I insisted that we focus on more immediate problems instead. Emma left to pick up the food and call Matthew, but the rest of us gathered around the antique wooden farm table that loosely defined the dining area in the large open-plan space. Hilary refilled wineglasses while Jane pulled an easel over from the corner of the room that served as Emma's studio. She tacked a large piece of drawing paper onto it, and then turned to us, marker in hand.

"Why don't we make a list of all the possible suspects?" she suggested brightly. "Then we'll divide them up and investigate." Jane taught math at a private school in Cambridge, and I suddenly had a vivid sense of what it would be like to be in her class.

Hilary groaned. "Good Lord, Jane. We're not your students, and this isn't *Scooby-Doo.*"

"But if it were, I'm not Velma," I said.

"I have the feeling it's going to be a very long night," said Luisa. She had crossed over to a window at the far end of the room, opened it wide, and lit a cigarette. I watched as she exhaled a stream of smoke out into the night.

"Come back, Luisa. How are you going to see the chart from way over there?"

"I'm trying to protect your unborn child from second-hand smoke," she pointed out.

"Oh. Thanks, I guess." Jane turned back to the easel. "Now, where were we? The suspects. Or should we start with the victims? What do you think, Rach?"

"Here's the way I see it," I said. "Gallagher was the primary target, but Dahlia knew something, or somebody thought she knew something, and that's what got her into trouble."

"Knew what?" asked Jane, scribbling on the easel.

"I don't know. But that brings us back to why anybody would want to kill Gallagher in the first place. His current and former wives have the most obvious motives. They both were in his office the day before he died, so they had the opportunity. And now Naomi's daughter probably gets an inheritance, and Annabel probably does, too, rather than getting divorced. Although, I'm not sure how much she'll actually get." I shared with them the tutorial Jake had given me on prenuptial agreements.

"Women are more likely than men to use poison to murder people," commented Hilary. "I read that somewhere. There's something very personal—almost domestic—about poison. It implies being close enough and trusted enough to access food or drink, or knowing somebody's habits well enough to poison him."

"But what about the work aspect of things?" asked Luisa. She crushed out her cigarette on the edge of the saucer she was using as a makeshift ashtray and rejoined us at the table. "You said yesterday that there was something off about this deal, Rachel. Could that be part of it?"

"I guess it's not out of the question, and I still think that there's something wrong with the Thunderbolt buyout," I said. I had already filled them in on the anonymous e-mail I'd received. "But, if somebody was trying to block the deal, and if the deal was dirty and Gallagher was involved, all he'd have to do is report him to the SEC. Poisoning him—well, it's like Hilary said. There's something sort of personal about it. Besides, it was a woman who pushed Dahlia, and as far as I can tell, I'm the only woman associated with this deal in any way."

"Then what would Dahlia know?" Luisa asked me. "If it was personal, rather than professional?"

"She's worked for him for a long time, so she knows both of the wives, and she probably ends up fielding a lot of his personal calls and correspondence, even though she shouldn't have to. Maybe she saw some papers that showed he was planning on divorcing Annabel, something like that?"

"But she said on her message that she wanted to talk to you about something she saw on the news," Jane reminded me.

"Maybe that was unrelated. Maybe she wanted to tell me about something else altogether?" I ventured.

"Could be," Hilary agreed. "But here's what I don't get. If it was one of the wives, how did she know to dress up like you when she went after Dahlia?"

The door opened just then and I gave an involuntary shriek. Being on the lam was still new to me, and I was a bit jumpy.

But it was only Emma, laden down with bags of food and, she said with a grimace, some "not-so-great news."

It had taken her awhile to locate a working pay phone "—I guess they just assume everyone has a cell phone now—" but she finally found one and got through to Matthew. He had another update from Peter: the police had returned to the apartment in the afternoon with a search warrant. It didn't occur to me at the time to wonder why Peter seemed to be spending all day in the apartment.

"A search warrant?" echoed Luisa. "That's really not good. That means they're serious."

"Rachel's innocent," Jane pointed out. "So there's nothing for them to find."

"Well, sort of," said Emma. "But I guess there was some stuff which, taken out of context, could be construed as evidence."

"Like what?" I asked.

"They took your computer, for starters."

"That won't be a problem. Peter seemed pretty confident he'd cleaned up the hard drive."

"It wasn't just your computer. They also went through your study and found something interesting enough to box up everything in there and take it all away. Do you know what they could have found?"

I didn't have to think very hard to answer this. Mostly the files in my study held financial statements and medical records—it was all fairly innocuous, unless you counted the number of cavities I'd had filled. But in my rush to leave this morning, I'd also left my briefcase, complete with my "insurance policy," the notebook I stored in its inside pocket, on top of the file cabinet. The most recent entries were pretty explicit regarding Gallagher's treatment of me and my reactions.

"That's not all," Emma continued. "They took your TiVo, too."

"My TiVo? There's nothing on it but Peter's *Star Trek* episodes and reruns of *Dawson's Creek*. And my entire *Forensic City* backlog—oh."

"Oh, what?"

"*Forensic City*. I didn't see it, but Jake told me there's an episode where somebody dies from a poisoned toothpick, sort of like how Gallagher died from the poisoned pencil."

"I saw that episode," said Hilary. "It was really good. I didn't figure out what happened until the very end."

"Was there anything else?" I asked Emma.

"Um, yes. One more thing," she said reluctantly.

"What?"

"Under the sink. In the kitchen."

God only knew what was in that cabinet—I'd been surprised simply to find usable dishwasher detergent the other night. It was probably all the same stuff that was there when I moved in. I'd always meant to sort it out, but I never really used the kitchen, so what was the point? I was fairly confident that my housekeeper kept it reasonably neat, but that was about the extent of it. "The woman I bought the apartment from was in her nineties. I have no idea what she might have accumulated," I said.

"Yes, well, she seems to have accumulated a nice big box of rat poison. With an active ingredient of potassium cyanide."

chapter sixteen

In the bleak wasteland that was my love life prior to Peter, I'd Googled the various romantic interests I'd had as well as the blind dates people foisted on me, and I'd been amazed by the wealth of information I'd found. For example, a few keystrokes had informed me that the charming venture capitalist I'd met at the Harvard Club was an avid collector of Beanie Babies, bidding them up aggressively on eBay. This knowledge promptly dashed any hopes I might have had for our future together, but better my hopes were dashed before we'd even started dating than after accidentally stumbling upon his Beanie Baby collection while looking for the bathroom in his apartment.

The Internet proved an equally fertile hunting ground for matters less romantic in nature. We were up half the night running searches on the names and topics that Jane had detailed on the easel, including Naomi Gallagher and Annabel Gallagher. We also did some Googling of the victims for good measure. The Web yielded a stockpile of information that we used to shape our plan of attack: everyone—except for me, of course—was out the door by nine on Thursday morning, eager to pursue their designated leads.

The good news was that cyberspace easily yielded recent reports on Dahlia Crenshaw's condition; the bad news was that while she hadn't been run over by the E train, she'd struck her head when she hit the tracks and had no memory of who pushed her. I was glad that she hadn't been seriously hurt, but it would have been nice if she'd been able to clear my name.

Naomi Gallagher turned out to be a relatively high-profile publishing executive—high-profile because she'd acquired and edited a bestseller about chemical and biological weapons of mass destruction. "Maybe she knows about more targeted destruction, too," Hilary suggested.

We also discovered a picture of Naomi and her daughter at a function at Caldecott Academy, her daughter's school, on the Caldecott Web site. "I know a woman on the faculty there," said Jane. "I met her at a continuing education seminar. And teachers at private schools like that always know the dirt on the parents. Why don't I look her up and see what I can find out?"

Annabel Gallagher had a substantial presence in cyberspace. "Figures," I said, when I scanned the results Google delivered, unconsciously echoing Naomi's reaction when she'd encountered her successor.

"What figures?" asked Emma.

"She was a model."

"Vogue?" asked Luisa.

"Victoria's Secret?" asked Hilary.

"No, she's not tall enough for that sort of thing—she mostly did catalog work. But still, a model." I wasn't sure of the precise origins of the term "modelizer"—many credited Candace Bushnell and *Sex and the City*—but just because it was on TV didn't mean it wasn't true. In fact, a whole subculture existed in New York of men who were obsessed with dating models, regardless of whether they themselves were model material.

However, the model in question here had been busily remaking herself as a socialite since she married Gallagher two years ago. Most of the references we found were about Annabel chairing benefits or otherwise attending charity galas. One reference was especially interesting, a gossip column blurb noting Gallagher's absence from an Annabel-organized function and speculating about "trouble in paradise." Personally, I didn't see how domestic arrangements with Gallagher could ever have been described as paradise.

"I'll take Annabel," said Emma with confidence. "I know the type, and I know where to find people who will talk about her." Emma's mother had been one of New York's social leaders for decades, so it wasn't surprising that she knew "the type," although she herself shied away from the social limelight.

Luisa nominated herself to try and figure out what Dahlia had seen on the news. "There's a video clips service that my law firm uses to track mentions of their clients on TV. It records all of the main broadcast and cable channels. I can scan the news programs and figure out what Dahlia wanted to tell you—maybe it was something relevant to the buyout."

"That's a lot of news," I warned. "Local and national news on the major networks. And then all of the cable news channels."

"What time did she leave her message?"

"Sevenish."

"So, it was probably the six-thirty national news on one of the networks. I'll start there, and if I don't find anything, I'll broaden the search."

It sounded like a thankless task, but Luisa seemed willing to do it, and I didn't have any better ideas.

Hilary, meanwhile, volunteered to use her journalist credentials and connections to investigate the investigators. "I can find out more about the case they're building against Rachel and see if they have any other leads."

"You just have a thing for police detectives," Luisa said skeptically.

"Two birds. One stone. Need I say more?" asked Hilary.

There was a flurry of activity as they all prepared to leave, which made the loft seem extra quiet and empty once they'd actually left.

Emma had made sure that the kitchen was well-stocked with essentials. I helped myself to a can of Diet Coke and some salt-and-vinegar potato chips. Usually I ate breakfast at the office, under Jessica's watchful gaze. She probably wouldn't have approved of this morning's menu, but that was the least of my worries.

I wandered around the apartment a couple of times and then stared out the window for a few minutes. I thought about getting back on Emma's computer to try to do some more research, but I wasn't sure what else to research. Nor did I have much of an appetite for Web surfing after an entire night spent online, searching every possible lead. Instead I turned on the television and flipped channels, but I couldn't concentrate on anything that was on, and Emma didn't even have TiVo.

Thinking about TiVo made me wistful for my own TiVo. I hoped it wasn't being handled roughly in police custody. I missed the rest of my belongings, too, especially my BlackBerry. It was strange to go so long without checking messages; I'd recognized that I was sort of compulsive about checking in, but I hadn't realized just how compulsive until I was no longer able to. I felt twitchy and anxious, and while I could chalk that up to being a fugitive from justice, the BlackBerry withdrawal wasn't helping. It was hard to suppress the sense that the world was moving forward without me.

I'd checked the new e-mail account Peter had set up a couple of times during the night, but it had remained empty. Still, it couldn't hurt to check again. It was the only thing I *could* check safely, and maybe checking it would stave off my withdrawal for a bit.

I sat myself behind Emma's desk and logged in to the account. I'd gotten so used to being disappointed that I was already steeling myself for an empty inbox. But instead I was rewarded with a message from Man of the People.

I eagerly clicked it open, hoping he'd been a bit more explicit this time around.

But he hadn't written anything at all—the e-mail was completely blank.

It was a good thing I was alone, because my yelp of frustration wasn't very ladylike. I scrolled down in disbelief, and then closed the message and reopened it. But there was still nothing.

Who was this peculiar anonymous correspondent, and why was he bothering to correspond if he wasn't even going to communicate? It was bad enough that it had taken him days to respond to my response to his initial e-mail, but to respond without actually responding just added insult to injury.

I was about to hit Reply and give him a fairly scathing piece of my mind when I noticed I had missed something.

The e-mail had an attachment.

I was even gladder now that I was alone, because it would have been embarrassing to have to explain to anyone that I'd overlooked the attachment the first time around. I double-clicked on the little paper clip icon and opened the file.

It was a photograph of three men, highballs in hand, standing in front of an orange-and-black banner that read Princeton Class of 1976, 25-Year Reunion. Actually, it looked to be a photograph of a photograph in a magazine, perhaps the Princeton alumni journal, because there was a white border around the picture and a caption underneath.

I didn't need the caption to recognize two of the men— they were slightly younger versions of Glenn Gallagher and Nicholas Perry. The third man was identified as Flipper Brisbane, apparently also a member of the class of '76. He looked too old to go by a name like Flipper, but if he let himself be called Flipper in the first place he was probably beyond help.

Man of the People had added his own caption to the photograph of the photograph: "They're in this together," it read.

While he at least hadn't sent me an empty message, and while the visual aid was nice, he still hadn't told me anything new. He'd said "they" had done it before in his previous e-mail, and I knew that Perry and Gallagher had collaborated on the Tiger buyout, too. I would have preferred more information about what, precisely, they were in together now, and maybe even some input about if it could possibly be related to Gallagher's death. I wondered if Man of the People even knew that Gallagher was dead.

Then it occurred to me that this Flipper guy might be more than an innocent bystander trapped in the same picture as Gallagher and Perry. I opened up a new browser window and typed "Flipper Brisbane" into the search bar. But the only results were links to sites about dolphins, pinball, and Australia.

I turned back to the e-mail and pressed Reply. I probably wasn't in the right frame of mind to be attempting persuasive communications, and Man of the People was only partially responsible for my current level of frustration, but I had to do something.

Enough with the cryptic e-mails already. Glenn Gallagher's dead, and they think I killed him, so unless you actually want to tell me something useful instead of confirming what I already know, stop contacting me. It's annoying, and I have a murderer to catch.
Rachel

I read over what I wrote. It was, perhaps, a bit terse. I thought for a second and then made a couple of quick edits.

Enough with the cryptic e-mails already. Glenn Gallagher's dead, and they think I killed him, so unless you actually want to tell me something useful instead of confirming what I already know, please stop contacting me. It's annoying, and I have a murderer to catch.
Best,
Rachel

The *please* and the *best* definitely helped.
Satisfied, I hit Send.

chapter seventeen

I sat in front of the computer for a while longer, waiting to see if my newly aggressive tone would inspire Man of the People to respond in a more timely manner, but no such luck.

By ten-thirty, I'd done several laps around the apartment, flipped the television on and off another three times, and checked for new e-mail repeatedly and fruitlessly. I'd also consumed two additional Diet Cokes, polished off the first bag of chips and started on another.

By eleven, I'd convinced myself that if I didn't get out of the apartment soon I wouldn't be able to fit through the doorway and that it would be safe for me to leave if I took the appropriate precautions. These consisted of ransacking Emma's closet in search of a fresh disguise, on the very off chance somebody had tracked me to Saks and there was security camera footage showing me going into the ladies' room and an Olsen twin coming out.

Fortunately, Emma was a bit of a pack rat. On a top shelf I found a platinum blond wig I remembered from a college Halloween party, when we'd all gone as different Madonna songs. Emma had been "La Isla Bonita" Madonna, complete with the matador outfit.

I skipped the matador outfit but pulled the wig on over my own hair, straightening it in the bathroom mirror and then taking a step back to survey the effect. It looked okay—like a bad dye job rather than a wig—but my eyebrows now looked strange, their dark red clashing with the platinum. Emma wasn't much of a makeup wearer, so I knew I wouldn't find anything useful like an eyebrow pencil in her medicine chest, but I did find a charcoal stick among her art supplies. With careful application, I managed to transform myself into a brunette who hadn't thought to dye her eyebrows to match her bad dye job.

I put an old pea coat on over the sweater and jeans Emma had already loaned me that morning. It was a good thing we were roughly the same size and that she had simple tastes; if it had been Hilary's closet, everything would have been either inches too long or far too skimpy, and if it had been Luisa's, I'd be too scared that I'd rip or spill on one of her precious designer garments to dare borrow anything.

A trip to the window assured me that the street below was quiet and seemingly clear of police surveillance. I stuffed money and my copy of Emma's key in a pocket, donned my sunglasses, and let myself out of the apartment.

I'd filled my MetroCard a couple of weeks ago, but I was still concerned that there were computers somewhere logging when the card was swiped at a turnstile and connecting the swiping to me via my credit card. But I also didn't want to be trapped in traffic with a potentially inquisitive or New York 1-watching cab driver. So I paid cash for a new MetroCard and took the subway up to midtown.

Hilary had said something interesting the previous night, but it was right before Emma arrived with food and the news about the rat poison so handily stored in my kitchen. The discussion had veered off in another direction, and Hilary's question had not received the attention it deserved.

How, she had asked, did Dahlia's attacker know to impersonate me?

I'd been thinking about this as I roamed Emma's empty apartment, and I still didn't have a good answer. Both Naomi and Annabel had seen me, but only in passing—they didn't know my name or how I fit in. Perhaps Dahlia had told one of them she knew something incriminating and that she intended to tell me, too, and perhaps one of them had thought that framing me while attacking Dahlia would be a nice way to tie up both loose ends, but there were still a lot of dots to be connected to make this line of conjecture work.

The more I thought about it, the more I kept coming back to the possibility that Gallagher's murder and the attempt on Dahlia's life could have something to do with the Thunderbolt buyout. It still seemed like Naomi and Annabel had the only obvious motives to do away with Gallagher, but if one of them wasn't responsible, and if the crimes were connected with the deal in some way, then maybe Gallagher and Dahlia weren't the only possible targets.

That somebody had gone to the trouble to impersonate me while seeking to commit murder had, in effect, made me a target, too.

And if I was a target because it was assumed I knew more than I did about this deal then the same assumption could be made about Jake, or even about Mark Anders. It seemed only fair to warn them they might be in danger.

I recognized that this was a relatively elaborate justification for getting out of the house, but this was about more than just warning Jake. I could use his help, too. He knew the context and the principals involved, so he might have insights that my friends couldn't have with their secondhand knowledge of the situation. And he'd be able to fill me in on anything that people might be saying around the office. He knew me well enough to know that I would never have done anything to hurt Dahlia. I trusted him not to turn me in to the authorities.

Besides, I would have lost my mind, as well as any ability to fit into my clothes, if I'd stayed cooped up in Emma's apartment any longer.

When he wasn't lunching with me at Burger Heaven, Jake favored a Halal vendor on the corner of East 52nd Street and Park Avenue. "You definitely can't get falafel like that in Chicago," he had said. I had never tried to get falafel in Chicago, but I agreed anyhow and regularly let him pick some up for me when he ventured out. I'd even trained him to ask for the appropriate amount of hot sauce, which in my case was more than anyone else found appropriate, even the vendor with his presumably spice-tempered palate.

By noon, I was perched on the wall bordering one of the fountains in front of the Seagram's building, about thirty feet from the vendor's cart. The food smelled good, but I was still too queasy from my salt-and-vinegared breakfast to think about lunch. I'd picked up a newspaper, and I scanned it while I waited, hopefully, for Jake to show up. Gallagher's murder and the attack on Dahlia were commanding prominent coverage, but while the articles referenced a missing red-haired suspect, I was relieved to see that neither my name nor photograph had been made public.

I was starting to doubt the wisdom of my plan, and I was also getting cold, when I spotted Jake coming from the direction of the Winslow, Brown offices, on the other side of Park. My distance vision wasn't necessarily my strongest asset, but the tilt of his blond head and his gait were distinctive. I put down my paper and rose to meet him, but instead of crossing the street he turned and headed north.

I followed him up Park Avenue. He was walking quickly, and with his long legs, I nearly had to run to keep up. I didn't want to draw attention to myself by actually running, much less by calling out his name. I was a block south of him and still on the wrong side of the street when a serendipitous red light afforded me the opportunity to cross to his side. I'd made it to the island in the middle when I realized Jake, too, was crossing the street, but to the side I'd just come from and a block up. I managed to backtrack before the light could turn green, but by the time I was heading north again he'd disappeared around the corner of 57th Street, heading east.

Where was he going? The only location of interest in that direction was Bloomingdale's, and Jake had always struck me as more of a Brooks Brothers type of guy. Throwing caution to the wind, I upped my pace to a jog, praying that my wig was anchored securely enough not to fly off and taking care not to make eye contact with anyone I passed.

When I turned the corner at 57th Street, I was rewarded with a glimpse of Jake entering a doorway at the far end of the block. I slowed my pace back down to a walk. I knew that doorway—it was to a Starbucks. I didn't see why Jake would go to a Starbucks on 57th Street when one had conveniently colonized the lobby of the building that housed Winslow, Brown's headquarters, but maybe he'd wanted the fresh air and the brisk walk.

I checked my reflection in a shop window and assured myself that my wig was still in place before I followed him inside, confident that I remained incognito. After the bright sunlight of the day, it took a moment for my eyes to adjust to the dim interior, made all the more dim by my sunglasses, and at first I wondered if I'd mistaken Jake for someone else entering the store.

But then I saw him.

He was sitting in a corner, in close conversation with a woman whose sunglasses were as large as my own.

But even with the sunglasses I recognized Annabel Gallagher.

chapter eighteen

I preferred my caffeine cold and carbonated, but Starbucks didn't sell Diet Coke, which seemed inhospitable, at best. I grudgingly ordered a frappuccino, and since the walk up Park counted as exercise, I also asked for an M&M cookie. I was becoming progressively more aware that the only barrier previously standing between me and substantial weight gain had been that I was usually too busy to fit every meal in. The surprisingly leisurely pace of fugitive life was giving me ample time for empty calories. I could only hope that all of the adrenaline boosted my metabolism, because I definitely lacked willpower.

My newspaper provided cover while I ate my oversize cookie and maintained a surreptitious watch on Jake and Annabel from a table on the opposite side of the store. Their discussion appeared animated. At least, she appeared animated in an upset sort of way, and he appeared animated in a reassuring sort of way. At one point he reached across the table and put his hand over hers.

From a distance, and with my sunglasses still on, it was hard to interpret the gesture. Was it that of a friend comforting a friend who'd just lost her husband? Or was there more to it, something more intimate? And even if there weren't more to it, how had Jake and Annabel become friends in the first place? And if they were such good friends, why hadn't they acknowledged each other on Monday, when we passed her on the way out to lunch? In fact, why hadn't Jake mentioned that he knew her when we were dissecting the likely terms of her prenup the day before?

Maybe it had been premature to write off my crush as entirely harmless. Maybe Peter had been right, and my feelings had gotten in the way of my judgment, and Jake's piece in this puzzle was more complex than I'd thought. It was becoming increasingly clear that I was completely lacking in emotional intelligence. Peter would be better off without me.

After about fifteen minutes and just as I was wondering if I could risk drawing attention to myself by getting up to purchase another cookie, Annabel stood. Monday's multi-brand ensemble had given way to head-to-toe black Chanel. She gathered up a trademark quilted handbag and let Jake help her on with a coat that had probably been made from an endangered species in a remote Asian village. I watched expectantly. Would they kiss? Hug? Shake hands?

But they did none of those things. Instead they contin-

ued talking for another few minutes. Then Annabel left—
there was no kissing, hugging, or hand-shaking—and Jake
returned to his seat. He pulled his BlackBerry from his
pocket and began pecking out a message.

He looked up as I slid into the chair Annabel had vacated.

"I'm sorry, but—"

"Jake, it's me."

His blue eyes widened. "Rachel?"

"Got it in one."

He leaned back. A slow grin crossed his face. "Interesting look."

"Yes, well, I heard blondes have more fun."

"How's that working out for you?"

"It's too soon to tell."

"You just missed Annabel Gallagher," he said. His tone
was easy.

"Actually, I didn't miss her at all. I was sitting over on the
other side and saw the entire thing. I didn't realize you two
knew each other." My own tone, in contrast, held more than
a note of suspicion.

He didn't seem to pick up on it. "I've known Annabel for
years. Believe it or not, I introduced her to Gallagher. We
dated for a bit when I was working at Ryan Brothers. I
brought her to a few work events, and that's when they met."

"Wait. Are you telling me Annabel dumped you for Gallagher?" I asked, astonished.

He shifted in his seat. "Well, dumped is sort of a strong
word for it."

"It sounds like a dumping." I knew I was being blunt, but

I was annoyed that Jake hadn't seen fit to share this before. Rethinking whether or not I could trust him really hadn't been part of today's game plan.

"Annabel and I were seeing each other, but it was still pretty casual, and then she met Gallagher and decided he was the one for her."

"So she did dump you for him." I said.

"It wasn't really a dumping."

"Well, I don't know how they define dumping in Chicago, but where I come from we call that dumping."

He threw his hands up in a gesture of mock surrender. "Okay. Maybe it was a dumping. But can you let a guy hold on to at least a shred of dignity?" He said this as if he was joking, but his cheeks were flushed. With a start I realized he was blushing.

"Sorry," I said, somewhat chastened. I hadn't meant to embarrass him.

"No, no, you're right. It's just that the truth hurts sometimes. And I guess, if you had to lay everything out in black and white, she did pretty much dump me. Only it was couched in the old 'I-hope-we-can-still-be-friends' brush-off." He looked up at me with the now-familiar rueful smile. "I get that one a lot. That and 'I-love-you-like-a-brother.'"

"But how could she go out with him after going out with you?" Jake was handsome and charming. Gallagher had been neither, and he'd been a couple of decades older than Annabel to boot.

"I can think of several million reasons."

"Yuck."

"It happens."

"But why didn't you say anything? You never even mentioned that you knew her."

"Look, when Gallagher moved over from Ryan Brothers, the last thing I wanted was people at the firm gossiping about him having stolen away my girlfriend. I mean, everybody already knew that I couldn't make my marriage work. I didn't want to be branded a complete loser. Could you blame me?"

"But you and Annabel stayed in touch?" I asked.

"She actually meant it when she said she wanted to stay friends. And it's probably pathetic, but for a while I hoped I'd win her back. In fact, I made a real ass of myself."

I couldn't believe it. He was blushing *again*.

What was it with men these days? First Peter, and now Jake. I thought only women were supposed to blush. But the blushing did restore my trust. It wasn't possible to fake that sort of thing.

"So what happened?" I asked.

"Nothing happened. They got married, and around the same time I met my ex-wife and moved to Chicago. When I came back to New York and realized I'd be working with Gallagher, we agreed not to let anyone at work know our history. Gallagher knew, obviously, but that was it."

I could understand why he'd want to keep it private, but it still seemed odd that he'd never mentioned it to me, at least, especially given everything I'd told him. "You could have told me."

"You were the last person I wanted to tell."

"What do you mean?"

He shook his head, not meeting my gaze. Then his eyes fell on my ringless hand.

He looked up at me, his expression quizzical. There was a long and awkward moment of silence. Then he opened his mouth to speak, but I beat him to it.

"So, what's Annabel's take on this entire situation?" I asked, before he could ask me any questions I wouldn't know how to answer.

"What? Oh. Annabel. Well, the murder has her pretty upset, obviously. I don't know how much she'll miss Gallagher, but she's convinced herself that Naomi killed him and is a homicidal maniac just waiting to take her out next. Plus, she's not used to being interrogated by the police."

"Welcome to my world," I said.

"But nobody really believes you did it."

"There seem to be a lot of people with various types of warrants who would disagree."

"Well, nobody who knows you believes you did it. But it's probably a good idea that you're making yourself scarce. The police do seem to be really gunning for you right now."

I told him about the alternative investigation my friends and I had launched. Now that I knew he and Annabel had more than a passing acquaintance, it didn't seem right to tell him that she was one of our primary suspects, but I did tell him about my concern, however far-fetched, that he and Mark could be targets, too. He raised his eyebrows but agreed that he'd be careful and would warn Mark to do the same. In fact, he even said he'd do some digging around for me at the office.

I also told him about my most recent exchange with Man of the People. "I think the guy's a crackpot. I don't know what he's trying to accomplish, sending me random pictures from the Princeton alumni magazine. Speaking of which, does the name Flipper Brisbane mean anything to you?" I asked.

"Flipper? That's really the guy's name?"

"Apparently. You're sure you've never heard of him?"

"I think I'd remember somebody named Flipper."

Maybe it was a dead end. Maybe Flipper Brisbane, whoever he was, just happened to be in that photograph by chance. If so, Man of the People had proven himself to be pretty much useless. I vowed to be more selective in my choice of anonymous correspondents going forward.

I gave Jake my new e-mail address. "You can use that to get in touch if you hear anything interesting. I've been staying away from my usual phone numbers and e-mail."

"Do you need anything? Are you okay for cash? Do you have a place to stay?"

"I appreciate your willingness to aid and abet."

"It must be the blond thing."

"Thank you for offering, but I'm fine. I'm staying with a college friend. She has a loft downtown."

"Emma the artist?"

There was a photo of my friends and me pinned to my bulletin board at work, one we'd taken a couple of summers ago, at Jane and Sean's house on Cape Cod. I'd forgotten that Jake had asked me about it once when he'd been in my office. "You have a good memory."

"The Furlong name is pretty famous, even if you don't know much about art. Besides, she looked cute."

"She is cute. In fact, she's beautiful. But taken."

"They always are."

There was another long and awkward pause.

"I should probably get going," I finally said.

"Me, too. I'll e-mail you, okay? And get in touch if you think of anything I can do."

"Thank you, Jake." He wrapped me in a hug, holding on for an extra beat.

I let Jake go before me, intending to wait a few minutes before taking off myself. The door had barely swung shut when a man at the next table got up to leave.

His chair had been hidden behind a display of mugs and packaged coffee beans when I'd been sitting across the room, and once I'd slid into Annabel's vacated seat Jake had blocked any view of him. His back was to me now as he walked away, but I recognized him from the suede jacket and the set of his shoulders. It was the same black-haired stranger who had been at the St. Regis the other night. The one Hilary wished had been buying her drinks.

We were only a couple of blocks from the hotel; it was possible he worked in the area, and that was why I kept seeing him.

But just in case, I rushed to follow him as soon as he was

out the door. I looked to the right and to the left when I reached the street, and I spotted him jogging west. Soon he was twenty feet or so behind Jake, and he slowed his pace to a walk, dropping in behind him.

Then Jake turned the corner, and so did the stranger.

There had been a lot of people in Starbucks, and there were a lot of people on the street, and there were any number of reasons somebody would go west on 57th Street and then turn on to Park.

But maybe my concern that Jake could be a target, too, wasn't so far-fetched.

Either way, by the time I reached the corner myself, I'd lost sight of them both.

I debated for a moment whether I was giving in to baseless paranoia before finding a pay phone and dialing Jake's cell phone. His voice mail picked up, but I left a message, warning him to be on the lookout for dark-haired men in suede jackets.

chapter nineteen

I arrived back at Emma's before anyone else had returned, which was a good thing, because somebody would probably have seen fit to lecture me about the risks I took in leaving the apartment, and Hilary definitely would have mocked the wig. She didn't believe in platinum blond for anyone but herself.

E-mail yielded no messages from Man of the People, nor did the Internet or TV provide any news of interest. I wanted to call Peter, but there wasn't a safe way to reach him, even if I had known what to say. By the time my friends started drifting in, the sun had set, I'd finished the second bag of chips I'd started that morning, and I was alternating between eyeing the leftovers from the previous evening and eyeing the lonely pint of aging Häagen-Dazs in the freezer.

Jane's timing was superb. I'd just concluded that cold pad Thai would add some much-needed carbs to my all-carb diet when her key turned in the door. She had stopped to pick up groceries and announced that she would be creating a Mexican feast. "We can have dinner and discuss what we all found out today."

This sounded like a reasonable plan, but I realized with regret that I wouldn't be able to do the promised meal justice if I started in on the leftovers. It was easier to make this decision once I saw that Jane had gone to the trouble of buying avocados and chilies for fresh guacamole. "Let me help," I offered. "I can smush the avocados. It will be both productive and cathartic."

She didn't even stop to think before she answered. "No. Even though there aren't any sharp objects involved, you carry some sort of food preparation hex around with you. Things always go wrong when you try to help."

"Nothing went wrong the time that I helped with the—" I searched my memory for a time when nothing had gone wrong but came up empty. I changed tacks. "How am I supposed to get better if nobody will let me practice?"

"I don't know. But you're not going to practice on any of us, let alone my unborn child."

Hilary came in right then and deposited her own collection of shopping bags on the table. "Speaking of unborn children, I picked up some tequila."

"What does that have to do with unborn children?" I asked.

"Nothing, really. But the good news is that because of Jane's unborn child, she won't drink, so there'll be more tequila for us." She pulled some limes out of one of her bags. "Salt or no salt, Rach?"

I looked at her blankly.

"For your margarita?"

Emma and Luisa arrived as Hilary was lining up drink ingredients on the kitchen counter. "Margaritas—perfect," said Luisa. "I think I'm going to need a stiff drink to get through all this." She held up a stack of hand-labeled DVDs.

"What 'all this' is that?" asked Jane, turning from the stove where she was doing something complicated with peppers and onions.

"Recordings of news programs on all of the major networks and cable news channels from six to seven on Tuesday night. It took the guy at my firm a while to dig them all up and put them on disk for me."

"So I guess that means we won't be watching *The O.C.* tonight?" asked Emma.

"It hasn't been the same since the first season," I said sadly.

"I know, but I still have such a crush on Seth."

Jane began assembling chicken enchiladas with a tomatillo and sour cream sauce, Hilary mixed a pitcher of margaritas, and Emma was deemed sufficiently competent to make guacamole. Luisa retreated to the window at the far end of the loft to smoke, and I sat and waited for dinner to be ready.

The margarita Hilary handed me was tart but mostly just strong. It only took a few sips before I found myself coming clean about my day's outing. I did get a scolding, as expected, with Jane tag-teaming Emma and Luisa. Hilary was more interested in the dark-haired stranger in the suede jacket, but this topic was quickly exhausted given how little I knew about him, so she turned back to Jake and Annabel.

"They were really an item? The same Jake from work, your Mr. Just-a-Nice-Guy-from-the-Office Jake?" she clarified.

"It's a small world, and he is just a nice guy from the office," I said. It didn't seem worthwhile to mention his questioning look and the awkward moments after he noted the absence of my engagement ring—I was still processing that myself. "His relationship with Annabel was apparently nothing serious, not to mention a long time ago," I said instead. "And it was actually sort of touching how embarrassed he was about getting dumped."

"I think it reflects well on him that he's able to stay friends with an ex-girlfriend, that she would turn to him when something terrible has happened," said Jane. She had a tendency to see most glasses as half-full.

Hilary used a finger-down-her-throat gesture to indicate that this sort of talk was likely to make her ill. She had a much more cynical view of human nature.

I helped myself to some chips and guacamole. "Enough about Jake," I said. "Jane, did you get anything on Naomi? Jake says Annabel's scared of her, that she thinks Naomi's the killer and is going to come after her next, but maybe she's just trying to deflect suspicion away from herself."

"I don't know about Naomi going after Annabel, but she does seem worth exploring further," Jane said. "I went up to Caldecott's and was able to track down the teacher I know without too much trouble, and we arranged to meet for a late lunch. That place is quite the institution, by the way. I think I was the only person who didn't arrive in a limo or a chauffeured SUV. And there was some serious bling going on with the mothers doing the dropping off."

"That was probably just the nannies," said Emma, herself a product of a Manhattan private school.

"Does anybody actually say 'bling' anymore?" asked Hilary.

"Nobody on the Upper East Side ever did," I told her.

Jane cast a wistful glance at the pitcher of margaritas. "Anyhow, I met up with Alex—my teacher acquaintance— at one, and it was pretty easy to turn the conversation to Naomi. I guess Caldecott has a couple of scholarship students, but for the most part all of the kids' parents are fabulously wealthy and are always trying to outdo each other at fund-raising events. Which makes Naomi Gallagher a bit of a rarity. Not only does she not have the resources to one-up anybody at the next school auction, this wasn't the first time she was late with the tuition for her daughter, and she's been pretty vocal about her ex-husband being the problem. She's referred to him as 'my ex, that stingy schmuck,' so many times in her conversations with the finance office that the term 'stingy schmuck' has become a running joke with the Caldecott faculty."

"That strengthens Naomi's motive," I said. "Her needing him to cough up his child support was nothing new."

"Wait, it gets better."

"What could be better than 'stingy schmuck'?" asked Hilary.

"On Monday afternoon, Naomi came in person to drop off the check she'd gotten from Gallagher. She must have come straight from his office. And guess what she said to the headmistress?"

"'I'm going to kill the stingy schmuck by poisoning one of his stupid pencils, so you won't have to worry about the tuition being late ever again, and then for good measure I'm going to push his secretary in front of a moving subway train?'" I guessed.

"Close," said Jane. "She said that she was confident that there wouldn't be any further problems with the tuition."

"That is pretty good. But it would be better if she'd said the part about killing him and Dahlia."

"Sorry, Rach. But I did find out where Naomi lives and also where she works. I thought I'd try to track her down tomorrow. She has a scary reputation—apparently the phrase used most in the faculty lounge is 'total bitch'—but maybe I can sound her out a bit more about her ex and about Dahlia. And about you, to see if she knew enough about you to frame you."

"Pregnancy is making you bold," said Emma.

Jane shrugged modestly. "What about you? Did you come up with anything on Annabel?"

She groaned. "I went to Janeane Proust."

"No!" I exclaimed, aghast. "I am so sorry, Em. I didn't realize that's what you were planning to do."

"Who's Janeane Proust?" asked Hilary.

"More like what. It's unadulterated torture disguised as an exercise class," Emma said. "But another Manhattan institution, and very popular with the lunching ladies crowd. Not that any of them actually lunch. It would counteract all of the time and money they spend at Janeane Proust. And on liposuction."

"Sounds like fun," said Jane.

"I think there's a good chance I may not be able to walk tomorrow—I barely made it home. You owe me an extended session with a qualified masseur, Rach." I reached for the pitcher and topped off her drink instead.

"Does it work?" asked Luisa.

"Anything that hurts this much has to work."

"You look really toned already," Hilary said.

"I did two classes in a row, just to talk to as many women as possible. And it was awful, like my mother's address book come to life, combined with intense physical anguish. By the way, when did the double air kiss give way to the triple air kiss?" Emma was usually on the quiet side. The pain and the margaritas had loosened her tongue considerably.

"I haven't even mastered the single air kiss," said Jane.

"Does Annabel go there? To Janeane Proust?" Luisa asked.

"Of course. Everybody who's anybody may not go, but everybody who *wants* to be somebody considers it a must. However, the word is that she's been slacking off of late."

"Slacking off at Janeane Proust?" I said. "Quel scandal."

"There's been a ton of gossip about her," Emma continued. "First, she spent a fortune on that new apartment, and the word on the street is that her husband wasn't pleased."

"Which street would that be?" Luisa asked, raising an eyebrow.

"Fifth, obviously," said Emma, "and selected stretches of Park, darling. Also, even though she's been skipping class, everyone says she's looking very well—that she's *glowing*. And you know what that means."

"She's pregnant?" asked Jane.

"She has a good facialist?" asked Luisa.

"No. That's code for having regular—and satisfying—sex."

"That you have to add the satisfying part is really sad," said Hilary.

"Presumably not with her husband?" asked Luisa.

"That's the implication."

"Maybe she's been seeing an ex-boyfriend on the side," Hilary suggested pointedly. Everyone looked at me.

"I didn't pick up on that vibe," I said. "She and Jake together...they really looked like they were friends and nothing more. I had more physical contact with him than she did."

"I've saved the best part for last," said Emma, thankfully before either Hilary or Luisa could make any of the responses I'd inadvertently set myself up for with my last comment.

"Which part is that?" asked Jane.

"The part about the divorce lawyer. Actually, lawyers. Annabel's been asking around for recommendations. Discreetly, of course, but none of these people are discreet. And the wife of Gallagher's own divorce lawyer is a Janeane

Proust addict. And a few weeks ago she started talking about renovating their Hamptons house."

While everything Jane and Emma had learned strengthened the argument that both Naomi and Annabel should be considered more seriously as suspects, we seemed to be the only people who were looking in any direction that didn't include me.

"I made some calls," said Hilary, as we lingered over the remains of the enchiladas. "I even dropped by the offices of a few crime reporters I know, and it sounds like the press coverage is going to heat up. The case against you is entirely circumstantial, but there are a lot of little things that look pretty convincing when you add them all up. And the bad news is that the investigating detectives are focusing all of their efforts on adding up those little things and on finding you. You were probably right to run, but that only confirms your guilt in their eyes."

"What's the good news?" I asked, trying not to sound as bleak as I felt.

"I bought an extra bottle of tequila, just in case one wasn't enough?"

"Matthew talked to Peter," said Emma. "And he didn't have anything else to report on things the police found. So that's good, right?" But she was reaching, and even she knew it.

"We just need to do more work," said Jane, striving for a confident tone. "I'll talk to Naomi, and Emma will get more dirt on Annabel."

"And maybe there's something on those DVDs," said Luisa. "We can start watching right now. Or as soon as I've had a cigarette." She took her case and lighter in hand.

"I'll contact some business reporters, too. To see if there's anything on Perry and Gallagher to follow up on," offered Hilary.

"Great," I said, but my voice sounded hollow. The gossip about Naomi and Annabel had been interesting, but it didn't change the fact that my situation wasn't good and appeared to be getting worse. The key that would unlock the answers to this puzzle was nowhere in sight. I tried to take comfort by reminding myself that at least I was safe here at Emma's, and at least I had the support of my friends.

"Oh, no," said Luisa from the window.

"Out of smokes?" asked Hilary.

"I'm afraid it's more serious than that," she answered.

We all turned to look. Flashing red-and-blue lights streamed through the window, illuminating Luisa's olive skin.

And then the downstairs buzzer sounded, long and loud.

chapter twenty

We wasted precious seconds gaping at each other in horror. A moment later, we could hear footsteps on the stairs.

"That stupid outside door," said Emma. "It never locks properly."

"Let's meet them on the stairs, and see if we can stall them for a minute," Jane said to her.

Hilary tossed me the small duffel bag we'd prepared for this possibility, and we raced to the back of the loft, to the bedroom.

"I'm really not a big fan of heights," I said as Luisa threw open the window to the fire escape.

"You might have mentioned that when we were devising your contingency plans," she answered.

"Don't be a wuss," said Hilary.

The fire escape hadn't looked so flimsy when we'd examined it the previous evening.

"Come on, Rachel," Luisa urged. We could hear voices on the stairwell, and more footsteps.

I took a deep breath and stepped through the window and onto the rusty platform. Behind me, they eased the sash down.

The fire escape faced out on an alley and the backs of the buildings that lined Vestry Street to the north. I knew that if I thought any more about it, I wouldn't be able to actually move, so I hoisted myself onto the ladder that snaked down the side of Emma's building and scampered the four stories to the ground.

I quickly realized that I was not the alley's only scamperer, but I really didn't want to think about what, exactly, the other scamperers might be. The hammer that we'd packed in my duffel bag did an admirable job of shattering the window in the back door of the building directly across from Emma's. The crunch of the breaking glass sounded tremendously loud, and I waited, frozen, for an alarm to go off. Miraculously, none did—at least, not an audible one—and the breaking glass didn't seem to attract notice, either.

I stood on tiptoe and pointed the small penlight we'd also packed in my duffel bag down the inside of the door, using the sleeve of my coat to protect my hand and arm from any remaining shards sticking from the window frame. In movies, people always just reached through the door and turned the knob, but in real life, this presupposed very long arms and easy or absent locks. I could see a dead bolt as well as another lock above the knob, but my own arms were too short to reach either.

Continuing to resolutely suppress any thoughts about the small moving shapes darting around disconcertingly close to my ankles, I dragged over a convenient trash can. It was rubber, not aluminum, and the lid dented and sank a bit when I climbed onto it, but it provided the additional reach I needed. I groped around and managed to unfasten both locks and twist the knob open from the inside. That done, I returned the trash can to its original location and dashed through the door before anything could crawl up my pants legs.

I was in a dark hallway, but a glimmer of light indicated where it met up with the front of the building. I exchanged the penlight for my Olsen twin hat, pulling it down so that it covered all of my hair. Turning back, I stole a glance through the now glassless window. I could see people in Emma's bedroom across the way, but they didn't seem to be examining her windows or fire escape. Somewhat reassured, I proceeded down the hallway, which opened on to a blissfully empty foyer.

A few minutes later, I was walking up Greenwich Street, wondering when the creepy-crawly sensation of rats and roaches nipping at my ankles would go away.

I tried to take inspiration from *The Pelican Brief,* in which the female heroine, Darby Shaw, found herself on the run, trying to prove a case while being hunted by assassins. Julia Roberts played Darby, but she looked fetching in all of her various disguises. She also had Denzel Washington, not to mention the good fortune to be on the run at a time when hotels didn't insist on credit cards for payment.

There probably were hotels in the city where I could pay cash, but I doubted that checking into that sort of hotel would do much to relieve the lingering creepy-crawly feeling. In fact, I feared that nothing short of bathing in acid was going to rid me of that.

I continued walking north, trying to figure out what to do next. This part of our contingency plan had been elegant in its simplicity, but it really only covered getting me out of Emma's loft. If the authorities had managed to track me to Emma's, it most certainly wasn't safe to call Peter, and my friends were probably being interrogated by the police at this very moment.

There was only one other person I could think to turn to. And while he was no Denzel, I couldn't begin to describe my relief when he answered my call from the first working pay phone I could find.

Jake was wonderful, calm and eager to help. "I'm at the office now, and I don't think it's a good idea for you to come here or to my place," he said. "The police are clearly extending their net to all of your friends, so they might think to go to my apartment, too. But let's meet somewhere and I can help you figure things out."

"Be careful," I warned Jake. I'd been thinking about the dark-haired stranger as I searched for a phone, cursing myself for not realizing what could happen sooner. I wasn't sure how he'd gotten to the Starbucks in the first place—whether he'd picked up my trail or had been following Jake—much less why he was following either of us, but once there I'd pretty much drawn him a map to my hideout. He must have tipped off the police to my whereabouts after eavesdropping on Jake and me.

It was dark enough that I risked taking a cab up the West Side Highway. It turned out that I had no need to worry; the taxi driver spent the entire ride chattering on his cell phone in a language I'd never heard before. Jake had suggested the West 79th Street Boat Basin. "The café's closed this time of year, but the outside part is open and it should be deserted. I'm leaving now, so I'll be there in fifteen minutes or so." Amazingly, he was still plowing forward on the Thunderbolt deal, even after everything that had happened and even though it had him and Mark slaving away at the office well after the technical close of business hours. At least being on the lam gave me a temporary reprieve from work

The driver pulled up to the designated taxi drop-off spot. He didn't look up when I pushed the fare through the slot in the divider but sped away, still talking on his phone, as soon as I'd slammed the door shut behind me.

I made my way through the pedestrian underpass below the highway and then around the shuttered restaurant and out to the rotunda overlooking the Hudson. As expected, it was deserted, and I crossed to the balustrade, pulling up my collar against the wind coming off the water. It was a crisp, clear night, and I would probably have even been able to see stars if they hadn't been obscured by the lights of the city behind me. A bright moon traced the outlines of the

buildings on the opposite shore, and the George Washington Bridge stretched across the river farther to the north.

I paced the flagstones, partially out of nerves and partially
to keep warm. The temperature had dropped considerably
during the day. As I waited, the initial quiet gave way to the
sounds of traffic from the highway and water lapping against
pilings. In the distance I could hear sirens, but they quickly
faded away. If it was more police, coming after me again, they
were heading in the wrong direction.

I squinted at my watch, trying to make out the time. It
was nearly nine, a full forty-five minutes since I'd spoken to
Jake. He may have been detained by something at the office, or perhaps he had trouble finding a cab. I hoped the
delay didn't have anything to do with the mystery man in
the suede jacket. I paced some more and tried to think
warm thoughts, but neither imaginary Caribbean beaches
nor imaginary hot chocolate could compete with the very
real wind chill.

Suddenly, I felt a rush of air whooshing past me and heard
a strange, high-pitched whine. Before me, a piece of the
stone balustrade dislodged itself and flew into the water.
Then I felt another rush of air and heard the whining noise
again. A few feet away, a flagstone dissolved into fragments.

Startled, I turned, holding up an arm to shield my face
against the wind, only to feel yet another rush of air and hear
another whining noise.

It was then that I noticed the smoke coming from my
sleeve. I lowered my arm to get a better look. A neat hole
had been drilled through it, fractions of an inch from the

arm inside. I could smell burnt wool, and the edges of the hole were still smoking.

Somebody was shooting at me.

I opened my mouth to scream, but nothing came out. I was too scared.

And then another flagstone dissolved at my feet.

chapter twenty-one

I was wrong. It didn't take an acid bath to get rid of the creepy-crawly feeling of vermin and beetles nipping at my ankles. Pieces of rock actually nipping at my ankles did the trick nicely.

My feet moved without conscious bidding. I ran to the far side of the rotunda and scrambled over the waist-high wall, landing on a narrow strip of dirt on the other side.

Panting, I took stock of the situation. The narrow strip of dirt was the only thing between me and the river's edge. Even if I were dressed for a swim, and even if I had any confidence that a swim in the Hudson would be healthier than getting shot, I doubted that I'd be able to last more than a minute in the frigid waters. But perhaps my would-be assassin thought that I'd taken the plunge. I didn't hear any additional flagstones exploding.

Very quietly and very slowly, I raised my head to scope out what might be happening on the other side of the wall. I was rewarded with another bullet, this one tracing a course through the very top of my Olsen hat. It was a very good thing I hadn't gone with a knit skullcap or a simple head-scarf. And it was too bad that I hadn't thought to buy a bul-letproof helmet instead of an Olsen hat. The smell of burned hair wasn't pleasant, but it was probably better than the smell of burned scalp or brains.

"Stop!"

The voice yelling this was vaguely familiar, but I couldn't place it. And if that was all that my unknown would-be as-sassin had wanted—for me to stop—simply asking in the first place would have been far more polite than starting off by shooting, especially since I hadn't been going anywhere, only pacing, when the shooting began.

"Who's there?" This came from another voice, one which I recognized immediately. It was Jake's, and he sounded sur-prisingly close, as if he was only a few yards away on the other side of the wall. He must have arrived on the scene between bullets.

I put my hands over my ears. The last thing I wanted to hear was the sound of Jake's head getting blown off.

"Put your gun down!" the first voice shouted.

Jake had a gun? That was weird. Unless it meant—

"Or I'll shoot," the first voice added, sounding closer this time. Again, I tried to place it. I definitely knew it from somewhere. It couldn't be the dark-haired stranger—I'd never heard him speak before.

"Who are you? And how do I know you're armed?" Jake countered. That was a stupid question. We knew the guy was armed because he was shooting at me.

Unless, he wasn't the one who had been shooting at me.

Which meant that Jake had been shooting at me.

After luring me to a nice, dark, secluded spot conveniently adjacent to a river that offered a superb outlet for body disposal.

I'd have plenty of time at a later date—at least, I hoped I would—to review the new heights of stupidity I'd reached and the countless ways in which I'd actively rationalized away all of the signs that had been pointing to Jake as a potential evil-doer. I did give myself a moment to wonder at his ability to blush on cue, and to seethe at the manner in which he'd manipulated me and my trust, but a more extensive session of self-flagellation would have to wait.

I steeled myself for another peek over the wall. This time nobody shot at me. The men on the other side were too busy with each other. My eyes found Jake easily enough. He was crouched in an archway on the interior side of the rotunda. He was wearing a ski mask of all things, but an inch of golden hair at the nape of his neck gleamed in the moonlight, as did the metal of the gun, complete with silencer, he was gripping with both hands.

The other guy was harder to spot. His voice was coming from closer to the entrance, but he kept himself well hidden as he and Jake debated which of them had guns and who was going to put his gun down first.

I spied another glint of light on metal just as the sound of a gunshot exploded in the night. The gun firing this time wasn't equipped with a silencer, the way Jake's was. I dived back behind the wall with a shriek.

But this shot hadn't been meant for me. I heard Jake curse and metal clattering along flagstones. When I poked my head over the wall again, I saw that Jake's gun now lay several feet away from him, and he was bent over, nursing one hand in the other. Apparently the other guy had pretty good aim.

My rescuer emerged from the shadows and sprinted across the rotunda. He grabbed Jake's gun, hurling it out over the balustrade and into the river. Then he turned to me. I started to duck, but he didn't raise his gun. "Rachel, get out of here!"

He, too, was wearing a ski mask. He also knew my name. And I still couldn't place his voice. I personally didn't own a ski mask and was feeling at a distinct disadvantage, both fashion-wise and in terms of having even the slightest idea of what was going on.

"Who are you? What is this all about?" I demanded, climbing back over the wall.

He turned to Jake. "Count to five hundred before you move. And I'm serious—I will shoot you if you follow us." He'd been yelling before and now he was using a loud whisper. Maybe if he used a normal tone I could place it.

"Come on," he urged, in that same loud whisper. "Let's go." He grabbed my arm and began running toward the entrance.

"I can run by myself," I told him. He let go of my arm but didn't slacken his pace.

We raced around the corner, side-by-side.

At which point I encountered another object, moving in the opposite direction but at a comparable velocity.

The impact threw me to the ground and knocked the wind out of me. It appeared to do the same to the other object who, upon closer inspection, was a man. He clearly hadn't been keeping up with *Men's Vogue* because he wasn't wearing a ski mask, although he was wearing a suede jacket. Which allowed me to identify him as the mysterious dark-haired stranger.

My rescuer in the ski mask had stopped running and paused to help me up. "Are you okay?" he asked, still whispering.

"I'm fine," I said, "but I don't think he is." The stranger was flat on his back, and in the dim light I could see a deep gash just below one eye. "We should get him some help." I didn't know if he was a good guy or a bad guy, but he was probably in need of stitches. Amazingly, I still had my emergency escape duffel bag with me, and I found a piece of cloth inside to press over the cut. It was a rag from Emma's studio, not a sterile bandage, but it would be a shame to let blood drip all over the suede.

Between the two of us, we managed to get the wounded and only partially conscious man into a standing position. We half walked, half dragged him the short block to Riverside Drive and into the lobby of the closest apartment building. There was a doorman there, seated on a high stool and watching a small television. When he saw us, he sprang to his feet. The three of us probably didn't look as polished as the building's usual visitors.

"Please—this man's been hurt. Could you call an ambulance?" I asked.

My ski-masked rescuer, meanwhile, deposited the bleeding stranger onto the stool the doorman had vacated. Without another word, he dashed back out the door.

"Wait!" I called. I dug through my pockets and pulled out some cash. Pushing the crumpled bills into the doorman's hand, I rushed to follow him.

But he was already nearly a block ahead of me, his figure receding in the darkness as he ran north on Riverside Drive.

chapter twenty-two

It was only ten o'clock when I reached the designated corner at Ninth Avenue and Forty-second Street, but it had already been a trying night, given all of the scampering and scrambling I'd been doing.

The corner wasn't very busy. At this time of the evening, the tourists were safely stashed away at the Broadway theaters nearby, and the Lincoln Tunnel traffic had long since thinned out. Nor was the corner as seedy as one would expect from Forty-second Street. Giuliani and then Bloomberg in collaboration with Disney and other corporate patrons had taken one of Manhattan's seedier neighborhoods and thoroughly sanitized it. The sanitization had its advantages, but as a fugitive from justice I felt that I'd earned the right to refer to Forty-second Street as The Deuce. It seemed unfair that the area was too clean and shiny to merit underworld parlance now that I was a member of the underworld.

I was getting a bit antsy and starting to worry that this part of the contingency plan had gone awry when a gleaming black BMW 645ci pulled up to the curb. I knew it was a 645ci because its owner had bored me on more than one occasion extolling its many tedious virtues.

I sidled over to the car, swinging my hips to the best of my limited ability.

"Hey, baby. Wanna date?" I asked.

Luisa looked up at me in disgust from the driver's seat. "Charming."

I shrugged. Forty-second Street was still Forty-second Street, after all.

She shifted the car into park and slowly unfastened her seat belt. "This is a very nice car," she said. She'd been reluctant for her car to be involved in our contingency planning and had only agreed after significant coaxing. When I'd reached her from a pay phone a half hour earlier, I could tell she'd been hoping that I would be able to arrange alternative transportation for myself and that this part of the plan would never go into effect. And telling her about being shot at had seemed to only heighten her reservations, masked rescuers notwithstanding.

"I know. You've told me that before. Several times."

"Technically, it's my sister's car. But it's only that the registration is in her name. It's easier that way, since I'm not a permanent resident. But everyone knows this is my car. I'm the only one who's allowed to drive it."

"I know," I repeated.

"It requires careful handling." She ran a loving hand over the polished wood of the dashboard.

"I'll handle it carefully."

She looked at me, and then at the dashboard, and then back at me. "I'm trusting you," she said.

"And I'm trustworthy." I tried to look like I was.

She locked her dark-eyed gaze on mine. "You know, you don't have the greatest reputation when it comes to driving."

Under normal circumstances I would have disputed this, but it didn't seem like a good time to argue. "It will be fine. Really," I said, in as convincing a tone as I could muster.

Reluctantly, Luisa opened the car door, making sure the bottom didn't scrape against the curb as she stepped out. I took her place, lowering myself onto the smooth leather of the driver's seat. But when I reached out to shut the door, she stopped me, placing a hand on its sleek frame.

"Remember, only premium gas," she said. "The most expensive kind you can find. I left extra cash in the glove compartment, so there's no reason to cut corners and buy the cheap gas."

"I will only buy the most expensive gas," I assured her, attempting again to shut the door. She resisted.

"And be sure to leave a space between you and other cars in parking lots. People are so careless these days."

"I will leave a space. In fact, I'll leave two spaces." I removed her hand from the door. "It will be fine. Really."

"You said that already." But she sighed and let me shut the door. "Call us."

"I will." I put the car into gear.

I could see her in the rearview mirror, watching. Her expression held concern, but I had every confidence that her concern was for the car and not for me.

I considered it a sign of maturity that I neither revved the engine nor made the tires squeal as I pulled away from the curb. I even used the blinker as I merged into the stream of downtown traffic.

Ten minutes later I was through the Lincoln Tunnel and in New Jersey, following the signs for Interstate Eighty West. The car handled so well that it seemed criminal not to floor the accelerator, but I held it to just above the speed limit. An encounter with the highway patrol would be particularly unwelcome this evening.

"Maybe we should stop at Ikea," suggested a voice behind me. "We could use some extra shelving."

I opened my mouth to scream, and this time it worked. A shrieking torrent of noise filled the car.

My hands jerked on the steering wheel, and I veered into the next lane. A horn blared out an enraged warning, and I swung back into my lane. A preadolescent girl gave me the finger from the passenger side of the minivan I'd nearly hit.

I'd had so many adrenaline surges in the last few hours that it seemed like my adrenaline supply should be exhausted, but it turned out I had plenty left. It coursed through my veins. I willed my pulse to slow as I struggled to get my breathing in check and my driving under control.

"Sorry," Peter said, clambering from the back into the front passenger seat. "I didn't mean to—"

"Give me a heart attack? Get us killed? What, precisely, didn't you mean to do?" I demanded.

"If you'd really had a heart attack, you probably wouldn't be able to drive," he pointed out, reaching behind him for the seat belt. "Speaking of which, it would probably be a good idea to pick a lane and stay there. The kid in the mini-van seemed sort of pissed."

"Where—how did—I mean, what are you doing here? And by the way, a little advance notice that you were hiding in the back seat might have been nice." Peter hadn't been part of the contingency plan, at least not part of the plan I'd authorized. Apparently some adjustments had been made to the plan without my consent.

"If we'd given you advance notice you would have kicked me out of the car while we were still in Manhattan. After all, we're in a fight, aren't we? Don't you remember storming out of the apartment yesterday?" His tone had shifted from playful to serious.

"Oh. That's right." I'd been indignant, but that was only temporary, a reaction to the shock of his sudden appearance. Now all of my earlier embarrassment and remorse returned. And I still didn't have the words—much less the confidence in my own emotional stability—to make everything right.

"Listen, Rachel, I've had some time to think about this, and I owe you an apology. I know you've been under a lot of stress, and I should have given you your space. And I should have trusted you, too. It was wrong of me to be so suspicious, and to make accusations like I did."

"But you were right about Jake—" I protested.

"Sure, I was right, but I was checking into him for all of the wrong reasons. You have a career that's important to you, and of course you're going to need to spend time with your work colleagues. And you had a personal life before, too, and that doesn't go away just because of me. I need to get used to that and to be more understanding."

"Um, well, actually—" I began, but Peter was on a roll. I had the sense that he'd been working on this little speech. I wondered if my friends had given him a list of talking points before smuggling him into the back seat.

"I've never been engaged before—hell, I've never lived with a woman I wasn't related to before—and I guess I've been acting sort of possessive. I don't know what came over me. You know that I'm not the caveman type. It's just that it's all so new to me, trying to fit myself into your life."

Given how little room I'd been making for him in it, that couldn't have been easy. I stole a glance at him, my eyes meeting the familiar rich chocolate of his in the dim light of the car.

I looked back at the road. "Actually, Peter, I'm the one who owes you an apology. And not just about Jake, even though you were the only one who had the good sense to really question him. You weren't acting like a caveman. You were acting like a normal part of a couple." I paused and took a deep breath. "It was me. I was acting like nothing had changed, like I was still on my own and didn't have anyone waiting for me at home. Like you weren't there."

He was silent for a moment. "Is that what you want?" he asked. "For me not to be there?" His tone was mild, so mild that it struck terror in my heart. How could he be so calm about such a momentous question?

"No!"

"No, you don't want me there?"

"No, of course I want you there!" Suddenly, that was beautifully clear. "But I'm not sure it's fair to you."

"What do you mean?"

"One minute I'm worried that things aren't going to work out, because they never do, and then the next I'm freaking out because my whole life is changing, and then you get caught in the cross fire, just because you have the misfortune to be there. Are you sure you want to sign up for that?"

"You'll grow out of it."

"What makes you so sure? How can you know?"

"I can't know for sure. But I do know I love you, and I want to be with you."

"Is it really that simple?"

"No, of course not. This is a first for both of us. It's bound to get rocky."

"I just—I just need to get used to it. I've never been part of a—a *partnership* before, and I'm still figuring out how it works."

"We could start with a lesson on the use of the first-person plural."

"What do you mean?"

"*I* mean that *we'll* figure out how it works," he said. Then he paused. "That was corny, wasn't it?"

"A little. Well, actually, a lot. But I liked it anyhow."

Out of the corner of my eye, I could see him digging something out of his pocket. It sparkled, even in the dark of the car.

I took my left hand off the steering wheel, crossing it awkwardly under my right arm and reaching it out in his direction.

The ring slid smoothly onto my finger.

Exactly where it belonged.

chapter twenty-three

I caught Peter up on recent events as we sped west along the Interstate. My friends were on the case in New York, reporting to the police that Jake had tried to kill me and urging them to treat him as a suspect. Of course, if you hadn't actually been there during the actual shooting, the whole story would sound preposterous, and I doubted that sharing it with the authorities would solve any of my problems. This was part of the reason I'd decided to get out of town. The other reason was that I—*we*—had research to do elsewhere.

Being shot at by Jake was enough to convince me that he was Gallagher's killer. My earlier gullibility may have been bottomless, but the blinders were officially off where he was concerned.

It was also enough to convince me that there had to be something going on between him and Annabel, regardless of what he'd told me at Starbucks, because it must have been Annabel who'd attacked Dahlia. Jake had put her up to it, of course, which was how she knew to disguise herself as a Rachel lookalike, and Peter had unwittingly let him know how perfectly the timing of my late start would align with Dahlia's commute. He used Annabel to set me up, both to deflect interest in him as a suspect and because he thought I knew something that would incriminate him. Then, when I eluded the police, he tipped them off as to where I was, helpfully aided by me, since I'd pretty much given him Emma's address that afternoon. In fact, he'd probably told the police about everything I'd told him all along: my "insurance policy," my love of *Forensic City* and my hate of all things Gallagher, not to mention my little jokes about murdering Gallagher by poisoning his stupid pencils. When I eluded the authorities again, he came after me himself.

But while I knew Jake was guilty, I didn't know why he'd done what he'd done. Was it to secure Gallagher's fortune for Annabel, and therefore himself, before Gallagher could divorce her? Of course, according to Jake, she was in for only a modest fortune whether she was a widow or a divorcée, but that could have been just another of his lies. Or was it even more complicated than that, related in some way to the intrigue around the Thunderbolt deal? Since New York was dangerous territory for me just now, the default option was to check into the latter. Poking around at Thunderbolt headquarters might help us answer, once and for all, if this entire thing was about the deal and, if so, how. Besides, I'd always heard that Pennsylvania was lovely this time of year.

Peter, meanwhile, managed not to say "I told you so" at any point in my narrative, and he seemed almost reluctant to add to the case against Jake. But he confessed that he'd continued to research him, in spite of our argument the previous day. He'd gleaned some useful information in the process, including that Annabel and Jake should be taken seriously as an item.

"Jake may have said their earlier relationship was a casual thing, but what I found suggests it was a lot less casual than he let on," he told me. "They went to a wedding together several years ago, and the wedding couple put their album online. The two of them definitely don't look casual in these pictures, and there's even a picture of Annabel catching the bride's bouquet. The caption said something about it being about time that Jake made an honest woman out of her, which implies that they'd been seeing each other pretty seriously for a while."

Peter had picked up some useful context about Jake's professional background, too. "I don't know what he told you about his previous work with Gallagher, but he worked on the Tiger buyout, too. I found an article from a trade magazine that mentioned he was on Gallagher's team at Ryan Brothers. The article was mostly about organized labor, and how the downturn in manufacturing has been forcing concessions from union leaders, but it talked about the Tiger deal and the Ryan Brothers team, and it mentioned both Gallagher and Jake by name, along with Perry. Are you sure that Jake wasn't part of whatever Gallagher and Perry had going on?"

"If he was, Gallagher did a pretty good job hiding it. He was just as abusive to Jake as to anyone else, practically. And while I recognize that I have no credibility now when it comes to Jake, there weren't any sidebars, any one-on-one conversations between the two of them that would indicate they were plotting. And if they were in on something together, why would Jake kill him?"

Unfortunately, all of Peter's Googling and my being used for target practice hadn't given us the remotest clue as to what Jake thought Dahlia and I knew that made us so dangerous, much less why he was so eager to set me up as his fall guy. Or fall person.

And while we had a better sense of who the bad guys were, we were still confused about the identity of the good guys. Neither Peter nor I could figure out who the two other men from the boat basin could be or even whether they were definitely good guys. Hilary had been put in charge of canvassing area emergency rooms in an attempt to track down the black-haired stranger. But I didn't even know where to begin to track down the guy in the ski mask with the familiar voice, much less how he fit in to this entire mess.

When I did find out, it was the biggest surprise of all.

Living in Manhattan can leave one jaded in certain ways. That man jogging up Lexington Avenue in a wig, Wonder Woman costume, and full makeup on a day that most certainly is not Halloween? He doesn't merit a second glance. The motorcades of visiting dignitaries are a nuisance and the thirty-dollar hamburger is a staple on menus around town. Spa pedicures for seven-year-olds aren't uncommon in certain circles, although I personally find this tacky. And the city is indisputably a shopping mecca, offering a broader array of wares displayed with more artistic flair than anywhere else in the world.

But there is one type of retail experience denied to Manhattanites that can thrill even the most jaded among us: the mass market chain store.

To be fair, there is a Kmart at Astor Place, but it's not the same as the Super Ks that sprawl luxuriously in suburbs across America, where there are no space constraints. I've also heard rumors of a Target in Brooklyn, but it seems to me that part of the experience is pulling off a highway and into a massive parking lot; not taking the subway or a taxi to another borough.

Peter had spent most of his adult life in California, so he was unprepared for my excitement when we pulled into the lot of a twenty-four-hour Sav-Mart somewhere in western New Jersey.

"Let's get a cart."

"We don't need a cart," he said. "There are spare clothes for us both in the car. A basket should do it. All we need are some toiletries and a couple of things to freshen up your disguise. The bullet hole in your hat is sort of conspicuous once you know it's a bullet hole. And have I mentioned how much I hate that hat?"

"But carts are more fun. In New York, they only have the mini carts, and they're impossible anyhow because the aisles are so narrow."

"When was the last time you bought enough of anything at a grocery store to actually need a cart?"

"Maybe I would do more grocery shopping if there were big grocery stores with big carts in the city," I countered.

"Fine. We'll get a cart." I had the feeling I was being humored, but that didn't really bother me.

We made quick work of picking up the basics, like toothpaste, soda and potato chips (it had been a long time since dinner, and I seemed to have developed a salt-and-vinegar fixation in the last forty-eight hours). But it was harder to plan for my new incognito look with so many choices presenting themselves.

Peter left me with the cart while he went looking for hats. He caught up with me in the hair dye aisle.

"No," he said, taking the box of Clairol Nice 'n Easy Natural Light Champagne Blonde I'd been examining and replacing it on the shelf.

"No what?"

"No, you are not dying your hair."

"Now you really do sound like a possessive caveman."

"I like your hair the way it is."

"But the way it is is sort of noticeable. Here," I said, pulling another box from a shelf. "This one's a rinse. It only lasts through three shampoos."

"Do you sincerely believe that this will be less noticeable than your natural color?"

"Not really. But if I'm going to dye my hair, I might as well try something really different."

"Looking like a Smurf would be different," he acknowledged.

"I never rebelled as a teenager." The prospect of changing my look completely was enough to make me forget why I wanted to change it in the first place.

After some debate, we compromised. I got the hair dye, but only the most temporary variety and in a shade called "caramel brown." "They might as well call it mouse brown," I grumbled.

"The objective here is to help you blend in," Peter reminded me, propelling the cart forward with one hand and me with the other.

"Blend, shmend."

He managed to get us safely back to the car without succumbing to the many valid arguments I put forth as to why the forty-eight-roll package of toilet paper was a steal at any price and how it would be tragedy to pass it up.

"You must be getting tired," he said. "Why don't you let me drive for a bit?"

"Did Luisa say that you could drive?"

"She encouraged me to. Everybody knows New Yorkers can't drive. None of them even have cars. In fact, I was supposed to make you switch places as soon as I could. I've been remarkably restrained for the last couple of hours."

"I'm a good driver," I insisted. "And that's very sexist of Luisa to assume that you're a better driver than I am." But I was tired, so I handed over the keys.

I dozed off immediately, waking up only when Peter brought the car to a stop. I sat up and looked around. We were in the parking lot of a motel.

"Where are we?"

"State College, Pennsylvania."

"There's really a place called State College? That's its name?"

"I guess there must be a state college around somewhere."

"I hope so. Otherwise it's just strange."

"Wait here. I'm going to check us in."

I managed to doze off again before he returned. The next thing I knew, he was opening the passenger-side door and nudging me awake. "Forty-nine dollars a night," he announced, holding up a key.

I was eager to get to bed, but forty-nine dollars seemed too cheap to be safe. A decent hotel room in New York couldn't be had for four times that much. "Was there a more expensive one?" I asked as we gathered our things from the trunk and made our way along the line of numbered doors.

"This is the most expensive one. In fact, it's the honeymoon suite."

"People honeymoon at motels in State College, Pennsylvania?"

"If you play your cards right, we could honeymoon here."

"What happens if I play my cards wrong?"

"You won't get the honeymoon suite."

"But we'd still be honeymooning in State College, Pennsylvania?"

"It's a win-win."

That made no sense at all, but he opened the door with a flourish, confident in his logic.

chapter twenty-four

It turned out that State College was named State College because it was the home of Penn State University, and it also turned out that the honeymoon suite featured a heart-shaped bed. In addition to being heart-shaped, it vibrated. And as if that weren't enough, there was a Jacuzzi, too. Not in the bathroom, but right there in the bedroom, across from the heart-shaped bed. And it came stocked with a nice big bottle of Mr. Bubble. A honeymoon in State College, Pennsylvania, might not be so bad.

We ended up not getting as much sleep as we'd intended, but I felt remarkably well-rested in the morning. I was still a murder suspect at large, but being back on a sure footing with Peter made that seem inconsequential in the larger scheme of things.

We checked out around nine, I with newly brown hair

and Peter wearing a trucker's cap that he'd purchased without my authorization at Sav-Mart.

"You look like Ashton Kutcher, circa 2003," I told him.

"Who's Ashton Kutcher?"

I didn't know where to start. Besides, if Peter was really that culturally illiterate, he was probably beyond help.

The first item on our agenda was to find a gas station as the needle on the fuel gage was hovering near the perilously empty mark. We found one on a broad street named, appropriately enough, College Avenue and opted for full-serve since it seemed like what Luisa would have wanted. The attendant complimented the car and our selection of premium unleaded, squeegeed the dead bugs off the windshield with aplomb, and pocketed our healthy tip with a big smile. People were friendly in the Keystone State.

Next we went in search of pay phones and Internet access. If we hadn't yet realized that State College was a college town, the presence of a Kinko's or Kinko's-equivalent on every other block would have tipped us off. We found one with a pay phone right outside its door and an empty parking space beckoning from across the street. I'd insisted on taking the wheel and was pleased to have the opportunity to combat the malicious rumors about my driving with a demonstration of parallel parking expertise. Peter, to his credit, offered only the occasional pointer, although his patience did seem to be wearing thin on my third, ultimately successful attempt to maneuver the car into the designated space.

He ducked into a nearby café to get a Diet Coke for me

and a coffee for himself while I went directly to the pay phone. The New York office of Luisa's law firm was sufficiently large and well-equipped to have a 1-800 line, which was particularly convenient in my present circumstances, although I was starting to get used to hoarding quarters. I didn't even have to talk to a real operator but could instead punch in Luisa's extension once I reached the main switchboard.

"How's my car?" she asked by way of greeting.

"Peter and I are fine, thank you for asking."

"Seriously."

"The car is fine. And we just fed it gallons of premium unleaded and had the windshield squeegeed. All by a trained professional."

"And you're letting Peter do the driving?" Normally, this question would have inspired a self-righteous lecture in which I challenged Luisa's assumption that Peter was a better driver than I. Today, it seemed wiser to opt for the harmless lie.

"Absolutely."

"You're lying, aren't you? I can hear it in your voice." I could almost hear Luisa raising one eyebrow—her preferred method of expressing skepticism—over the phone.

I'd thought it would be safe enough long distance but clearly not. I tried to change the subject. "What's going on back there? What's the update?"

"I'll give you the update if you promise to let Peter drive from now on."

I crossed my fingers behind my back. "All right, Peter

will be the designated driver. So what's the news? Anything good?"

"Not really, but since we're talking about news, you should probably know that you're it."

"What do you mean, I'm it?"

"The police went public with your name, and you're in every paper this morning, and on TV, too."

For once I was glad to be without my phone. I could only imagine the messages my parents were leaving on it.

"Don't worry," Luisa said, as if she knew what I was thinking. "Emma already called your parents and told them not to panic. And Jane had a long talk with your grandmother about how many children you should have. They agreed on five."

"What are they saying? In the papers and on the news?"

"They're describing you as 'wanted for questioning.' And there's a picture of you, too."

"Which picture?"

"What do you mean, which picture?"

"Is it a good picture?"

"I think it's from your Winslow, Brown ID. It's very professional. You're wearing a suit."

"Oh. Do you think you could get them a better one?" The Winslow, Brown picture was sort of blurry, and they hadn't given me a chance to even smile before they snapped it.

"Get who a better what?"

"The press. I mean, if your picture was going to be all over the news, wouldn't you want to make sure that it was at least a good picture?"

"I'm going to pretend we're not having this discussion."

"Okay. What else is going on? Did you tell the detectives about Jake trying to kill me last night?"

She sighed. "We tried, Rachel, we really did. But they're not biting. Just because they didn't find you at Emma's doesn't mean that they don't suspect us all of aiding and abetting. Especially since we couldn't exactly tell them how we found out about Jake shooting at you. It wasn't the most credibility-building of exercises."

My expectations had been low on this front, but it was still disappointing news. "What about the mystery man in the suede jacket? Any news on him?"

"Hilary checked all of the area emergency rooms but had no luck. However, she's moved on to Plan B."

"What's Plan B?"

"She figures that if this man has been following Jake, she'll be able to locate him by following Jake, as well."

I envisioned Hilary following the man following Jake. "It will be like a parade. How will Jake not catch on?"

"Hilary said she'd be subtle." I had a feeling that Luisa's eyebrow had shot up again as she said this.

"Hil's never been subtle in her life."

"I needed to be here to take your call, and it seemed too risky to have Emma do it since the police still seem to think she was harboring you at her loft, and that only left Jane."

"Even if she were ten months pregnant, Jane could be more subtle than Hilary."

Now I could almost hear Luisa shrug. "True. But Hilary insisted."

"Are you sure there isn't even a little bit of good news?" Thus far, things were looking sort of dire.

"I don't know if this is good, but Jane spoke to her teacher friend and it looks like Naomi Gallagher had an alibi for when Dahlia was attacked, so she's definitely out of the running."

"What kind of alibi?"

"A Caldecott Parents' Association meeting. During which Naomi engaged in heated debate with one of the other mothers about uniform hem lengths or something equally controversial. Apparently blows were nearly exchanged. So it's not as if she slipped out after the meeting started to go attack anyone."

"Well, I guess it's nice to have one loose end tied up."

"And in the spirit of tying up loose ends, we were up most of last night going through the TV recordings from the other night, to see if we could figure out what Dahlia had seen."

"Anything interesting?"

"Nothing leaped out at us, unfortunately. But we made a list of the stories. Do you have time for me to read it to you? It's sort of long."

I'd been staring at the door of the copy shop while she spoke, and it presented a handy solution. "Why don't you fax it to me?"

"Under what name?"

I no longer had my Olsen hat for inspiration. "How about Underhill?" I suggested.

"Why Underhill?"

"You know. From *Fletch*."

"What's *Fletch?*"

I didn't know how to respond to this. Luisa had officially trumped the cultural illiteracy of my fiancé. Even taking into consideration that she had grown up on a different continent, her lack of familiarity with the classic works of Chevy Chase was astounding. However, this was not a deficit that could be solved over the phone today. Instead, I gave her the number from the sign on the door and promised to check in later. I hung up just as Peter arrived.

"Anything?" he asked, handing me a can of soda.

"Nothing good."

He leaned in to kiss me.

"Except that," I added.

I left him at the phone and went inside, where I found the expected bank of computers. I fed a ten-dollar bill into a vending machine to purchase a debit card, selected a station in a quiet corner, inserted my card into the reader, and opened up a Web browser to log into my new e-mail account.

The account was less than a week old but it had already been discovered by spammers. It took me a few minutes to delete all of the ads for homeopathic aphrodisiacs, after which I was left with two real messages. The first was from Man of the People. That was a relief—I'd been worried that yesterday's less than gracious response might have alienated him, and I'd since realized that any lead, however tenuous, we could get on Thunderbolt could only help. We needed Man of the People to come through for us.

His e-mail was, as usual, more cryptic and less informa-
tive than I would have liked.

They killed Gallagher? I hadn't realized just how dangerous they are. I can't risk getting you involved in this.
I won't e-mail again. And you should take care, now that
we know what they're capable of.

Wasn't Gallagher part of the "they" in the first place? And
wasn't it a little late to be worrying about my involvement?

"What have you got?" asked Peter, pulling a chair over
from another work station.

I showed him.

"Well, at least he returned your last e-mail. And at least
we know he thinks Gallagher got killed because of this deal."

"Sure, but he probably doesn't know about Jake and Annabel and that side of the story, either."

"We should still e-mail him to tell him that we're on our
way to Thunderbolt and ask him to help us get to the bottom of things. If he's actually involved with Thunderbolt
and lives in the area, like we think, maybe he'll even agree
to meet with us in person."

But when we sent an e-mail off, saying just that, we got
a message back almost instantly, saying something about an
Unknown User.

"What's wrong?" I asked.

Peter examined the text of the message and shook his
head. "He canceled the account. We can't e-mail him there
anymore."

I groaned. "So, we've come all this way and now we can't even contact our most promising source?"

"We'll figure something out," he said. "Besides, it wasn't like he was ever that promising as a source."

"Yes, but at least we had one."

"Also true."

The other message was from Jake, and that he'd e-mailed me at all was just plain bizarre.

"What did Jake have to say for himself?" Peter asked.

"I wasn't sure if I should open it. Could he have tagged it in some way, so that opening it could tell him where I am?"

"There are ways to do that, by inserting a code that would communicate back to the original e-mail server, but he would probably need a few programmers to help him do it. It should be fine."

I clicked on the Read icon and opened Jake's message.

Are you all right? It took me longer to get to the boat basin than I expected, but then you weren't there. I waited for an hour. What happened? Is everything okay?

I stared at the words in disbelief. Did Jake actually think that I hadn't recognized his voice, that I didn't know that it had been him under that ski mask? Even recognizing that I'd been playing right into his hands for days, he couldn't possibly think I was still clueless.

"The nerve of that guy!" said Peter. "He tries to shoot you, and then he tries to pretend it never happened? Who the hell does he think he is?"

"We should write back and tell him what we think of him and his nerve."

"I'd like to show him what I think of him and his nerve." Peter's hands had clenched into fists. I found this endearing.

"But he's not here, so we should write him back and tell him."

"I'd like to, but we shouldn't, even using the resend service. We don't want to give him any sense of what you're up to, even if it's only checking e-mail."

"You're probably right," I said, disappointed.

"Unfortunately, yes."

"They should have a Kill function on e-mail. You know, Reply, Reply all, Kill, Kill all."

"That's not a bad idea." He stood up and returned his chair to its original place. "I need to make one more call, and then we'll hit the road, okay?"

"Sure," I said, distracted. I was still fretting about Man of the People while simultaneously fuming about Jake's e-mail.

It didn't occur to me to wonder who Peter could be calling.

chapter twenty-five

I lost the coin toss, even after we made it two out of three and then four out of seven, so Peter was at the wheel when we left State College behind. As co-pilot, my principal role was to navigate based on the route Peter had printed out from MapQuest, but since I'm not actually capable of reading maps, I held the wheel steady while Peter consulted the printout.

I was also in charge of the radio, which left a lot to be desired in rural Pennsylvania. It was unlike Luisa to skimp on luxury features like satellite radio, but skimp she had, leaving us at the mercy of local tastes, which seemed to lean toward Christian rock and bluegrass.

Peter and I had never spent much time in a car together before, and I was concerned to find that in addition to being culturally illiterate, he was woefully ignorant regarding appropriate behavior on any road trip lasting more than an hour. For example, he believed in finding a radio station, preferably NPR, and sticking to it. This was, of course, wrong, even assuming one could find NPR. The proper approach was to make continuous use of the handy seek function to ensure that we weren't missing something better on another station. When we did find something better, it was customary to sing along.

The fast food rule was new to Peter, as well. He thought that for lunch we would pull off the highway and locate a quaint diner where we could enjoy local Amish Country delicacies like apple butter and pretzels, when it's widely understood that being in a car for more than an hour automatically entitles one to eat fast food. The grease and salt content of the fast food to which one is entitled is a function of just how much time one has spent in the car. I'd assumed that all Americans of my generation possessed this knowledge, much as they knew the words to *Free to Be You and Me* and that drinking soda after eating Pop Rocks could be fatal, but Peter seemed to be the exception.

"I never knew you were such a McDonald's fan," he commented while we waited our turn in the drive-through line.

"You're not?" I asked, but I wasn't really paying attention. I was absorbed in the Big Mac versus Quarter Pounder with Cheese decision. The Big Mac had the advantage of being, well, big, but the Quarter Pounder was tasty in its own way and left more room for fries.

"Not so much," he admitted.

This got my attention. "Are you a Communist?"

"Not liking McDonald's makes me a Communist?"

"I don't know which is cause and which is effect, so it could be the other way around." A car behind us honked. "Look, it's our turn. Do you want me to order for you?"

Peter insisted on ordering for himself and asked for a salad, which made me really wonder if he was some sort of Soviet plant, like Kevin Costner in *No Way Out,* who hadn't been repatriated after the collapse of the Berlin Wall. I reminded myself that I'd met his entire extended family and spent long hours with his very American mother examining a photographic record that began with Peter in the womb, but it was the gusto with which he polished off the remainder of my Big Mac and half my fries that ultimately convinced me he wasn't secretly named Yuri.

Twenty minutes later, and feeling only slightly queasy from lunch, we were back on the highway. The drive would probably have been scenic at a different time of year—there were a lot of trees and rolling hills and red barns—but in mid-March the trees were bare and the hills and barns were blanketed with tired, graying snow.

It was early afternoon when we reached the outskirts of Pittsburgh and the rural flavor began to give way to rusting industrialism. MapQuest got us to where we were going without too much trouble—it only tried to make us go the wrong way up one one-way street—but since Peter had the sense of direction I so sadly lacked, he was able to improvise, steering a confident course through an area that was a mix of working factories, abandoned factories, and empty lots.

"That must be it," he said eventually, giving the map a final glance and pulling up to a corner. Across the street and to the right was our destination, the headquarters of Thunderbolt Industries. It looked pretty much like what it was: a rust-belt manufacturing plant. The building itself was a sprawling architectural hodgepodge of dingy red brick, dingy cinder block, and dingy concrete. The only shiny part was a glass-walled addition, clearly an afterthought. It extended awkwardly from one side of the factory and likely housed the executive offices. From the street, the complex appeared to be the size of a football field, but it was hard to tell how far back it extended. Only two of the many smokestacks were emitting smoke, a testament, no doubt, to the slump the company was in, and the potholed asphalt parking lot was only half-full.

Minivans seemed to be the vehicles of choice for Thunderbolt employees; in fact, they seemed to be the vehicle of choice for everyone west of the Hudson. As a result, one car really stuck out, and it gave me a sense of just how much Luisa's car must have been sticking out during our entire trip. It was a BMW 645ci, and it occupied a space directly in front of the glass annex. The BMW in the parking lot was red instead of black, and it had a hard top while Luisa's was a convertible, but maybe its owner used another car in better weather.

"I'll bet you anything that's Perry's car," I said, pointing it out to Peter.

"Why would I bet you on that? I never met Perry. How would I know what kind of car he'd drive? Besides, it's red. Does that make it a Communist car? Is Perry a Communist?" Peter was still a bit testy from the Yuri discussion.

"Hardly—I think he's pretty solidly on the capitalist pig end of the spectrum. In fact, I would have pegged him as a limousine type of guy. Or maybe just a Mercedes, but with a driver, so that he can sit in the back and read the paper and act snooty. But definitely not the sort of guy to do his own driving."

"Maybe he's more of a man of the people than you're giving him credit for—" Peter caught his own words and laughed. "Hey—maybe he's our guy."

"You mean, he's been sending me annoying e-mails in an attempt to derail his buyout? Somehow I don't think so, even if he does drive his own car."

"Me, neither. Which is too bad, because we still don't know who or what we're looking for, exactly, and we're out of luck if we actually want to get in. There's a security booth at the gate."

"We knew there probably would be," I answered, but I was still disappointed. I'd held the faint hope that I'd be able to walk in and pull an Erin Brockovich (minus the cleavage, unfortunately), talking my way into a look at whichever files held incriminating evidence and soliciting suggestions from helpful employees as to who Man of the People might be. Our revised, Man-of-the-

People-less plan had allowed for us being unable to gain access to the building, but it had seemed worth a try. "Let's see if maybe there's a back way, just in case there is and it's open."

"Sure." Peter put the car in gear, and we cruised around the block. The fenced perimeter yielded a couple of additional entrances, but while these lacked security guards, the steel gates were the sort that could only be opened with a keycard. We considered parking the car and walking in, but it seemed unlikely that we'd make it very far into the building unnoticed given the signs of security we'd seen so far.

We'd nearly completed our circuit and were passing the front entrance when I noticed something. "Peter—wait. What does that sign say?" He slowed the car and followed my gaze with his own.

"You can't read that sign?"

"I know there's a sign and that it has words on it."

"You can't read that sign and you've been driving? When was the last time you had your eyes checked?"

"I had them checked."

"In the last decade?"

"Sure."

"You're lying, aren't you?" I tried to look like I wasn't, but it was becoming all too clear that my lying skills were subpar. "Listen," he said, "I'll tell you what the sign says, but there's no way that you're driving again until you get glasses."

"Fine." This wasn't really a lie; I figured that I could re-negotiate the driving clause later.

Peter read the notice aloud:

SPECIAL SHAREHOLDER MEETING
VOTE ON PROPOSED SALE OF COMPANY
SATURDAY, MARCH 18TH
TEN A.M.

"Well, that's convenient," he said.

"Among other things." Mostly it was just incredibly fast. How had they had been able to pull the deal together in a week? Especially with everything that had been going on? "Perry must have called a special session of the board of directors and muscled the buyout proposal through. Now they're putting it to a final vote."

"That was quick work."

"Ridiculously quick. Jake mentioned that Perry was eager to keep moving this forward—he didn't even skip a beat after Gallagher kicked the bucket—if anything, he accelerated the schedule."

"Why the rush?"

"I don't know. We—the firm—like to turn things around quickly, but this is unprecedented. Less than a week from an initial proposal to a shareholder vote? Jake must have been killing himself the last few days to get it done. At least, when he wasn't trying to kill other people."

"What's in it for Jake, then?"

"I don't know," I said again, frustrated.

"Are you sure he's not in on it somehow?"

"I'm not sure of anything at this point."

"Does all of this mean that Jake will be here tomorrow?"

"He should be," I said. "Now that Gallagher's not avail-

able, Perry would want someone on hand to answer questions, maybe even to present the deal to the shareholders in
the first place."

"I'd like to have a little talk with him."

"Me, too. Does your little talk involve pepper spray and
jumping up and down on his face while wearing cleats?" I
was a firm believer in holding a grudge. It was going to be
a long time before I got over Jake treating me like a me-
chanical duck in his personal shooting gallery, not to mention assuming that I'd be too dense to realize it was him.

"I was thinking more along the line of a baseball bat and
his knees."

"That could work."

chapter twenty-six

Beating up Jake would have to wait until the next day. I'd read somewhere that the ability to delay gratification is a sign of maturity, and Peter and I were nothing if not mature.

We had been prepared to be unable to gain access to Thunderbolt's premises, so our plan was to find the local hangouts frequented by Thunderbolt's employees. There we intended to casually engage happy-hour patrons in discussion of Thunderbolt, Perry, the proposed buyout, and even Tiger Defense in a last-ditch attempt to track down Man of the People and to uncover any possible clues as to what, precisely, was so dirty about this deal.

As plans went, we recognized that it was fairly lame and that its odds of success were relatively low. It also relied on social skills that neither I nor Peter really had, but we hadn't been able to come up with more attractive alternatives. I was becoming resigned to the ways in which being on the wrong side of the law, however unjustly, limited one's ability to pursue justice effectively.

We still had a few hours to kill between the end of the workday and the beginning of our pub crawl, so we drove off in search of yet another pay phone and more Internet access. While State College had offered nothing but copy shops and Internet cafés, here the pickings were slim. We finally located a public library and pulled into its parking lot. The library's architect appeared to be from the same school as the architect responsible for Thunderbolt's plant, but the building compensated for its ugliness with a line of computer terminals inside and a pay phone in the back corridor near the restrooms.

I called Luisa first to see if there had been any new developments.

"Did you get the fax?" she asked. "Did any of the stories mean anything to you?"

I'd scanned the list she'd sent in the car, and nothing had struck me as particularly relevant. I told her as much, feeling apologetic because the list had clearly represented a lot of television watching and Luisa was unabashed in her conviction that television was directly responsible for the decline of Western civilization.

"You mean we watched all of those vile blowhards on Fox News for nothing?"

"But you got to see Anderson Cooper, too. He's not a vile blowhard."

She harrumphed her reply.

"What's going on with Hilary? Has she found the guy in the suede jacket?"

"Last I heard, she was watching Jake and Annabel having a cozy-looking lunch and was pissed that she was skipping her own lunch to do so. But there was no sign of the man following Jake, and I doubt that Hilary would have missed him if he was there. She has a good eye for attractive mysterious strangers."

I told Luisa about Jake's e-mail, and she was appropriately incensed about his attempt to play the innocent. Then she gave me a new number to call for my next check-in. "The IT department here hooked me up with a temporary mobile phone. This number should be safe for a day or two."

Peter was waiting, so I thanked Luisa and ended our call, assuring her that we'd get in touch later that evening. I left him loading quarters into the phone and went to one of the computer terminals to check my new e-mail account in the vain hope that Man of the People had reconsidered. But all of the e-mails that had accumulated since that morning were spam.

I closed out of e-mail and took a moment to scan the latest headlines on the Web. I seemed to be in luck, as a major earthquake had struck Kazakhstan just a couple of hours ago, completely eclipsing me as a story. It seemed wrong that an earthquake was working in my favor, but there wasn't much I could do about it now. I made a mental note to donate to a relief fund as soon as I regained access to my bank account.

I stood up and stretched, still cramped from the long car ride. Across the room, I could see down the back corridor and Peter's profile as he spoke on the phone. A fresh wave of gratitude washed over me. This couldn't have been a convenient time for him to ditch work and go on the lam with his wayward fiancée. Peter glanced up and, catching my eye, gestured to indicate he needed a few more minutes before tipping the brim of his trucker's cap in my direction. I hoped he wasn't getting too attached to this new accessory. Gratitude aside, there was no way I was going to let him keep wearing something that silly-looking after all this was over.

I returned to my chair in front of the computer. My conversation with Luisa had made me wonder if perhaps I'd accidentally missed something important on her list of stories. I might as well use the downtime to take another look.

The items on the fax had been carefully grouped, probably by Luisa or Jane, who were the most structured thinkers among my friends. The first heading was International and included a long list of stories about events on other continents: armed insurgencies in the Middle East, political turmoil in Eastern Europe, and trade tensions among Asian nations. I was fairly confident that none of these stories had inspired Dahlia's fateful call to me and had skimmed through this list rapidly in the car.

The next heading was National/Politics, and I'd skimmed through that section rapidly as well, focusing my attention on the category labeled Business, thinking that it would be the most likely to yield useful information. I looked over the stories in this category again, and I even pulled up a few related articles on the Internet, but nothing seemed connected to the mess I'd found myself in.

A quick visual check showed me that Peter was still on the phone, so for lack of anything better to do I turned back to the stories grouped under National/Politics to give them more careful consideration, typing relevant keywords into the search bar. But no matter how I tried, I couldn't figure out why Dahlia would want to tell me about trends in student test scores, the death of a famed civil rights leader, drug use in suburban America, or Congressional debate regarding proposed health-care legislation. It seemed like Luisa really had had to watch those vile blowhards on Fox News for no good reason.

The final item on the list was about the progress of a new appropriations bill through the Senate Armed Forces committee. The futility of the entire effort made me sigh as I typed in "Senate Armed Forces" and "appropriations" and hit enter. With another sigh, I clicked on the first article returned by the search, a link to a *Washington Post* article from Tuesday's edition with the headline: Senate Armed Forces Committee Debates Appropriations Bill.

I was already halfway through the article before I realized that there was a familiar name in the very first paragraph. I returned to the beginning and read it again, more carefully this time.

The Senate Armed Forces Committee continued its debate today on the new appropriations bill. "We are confident that we will ultimately deliver a bill that provides our military with the resources it needs to protect American interests at home and abroad," said Committee Chair Senator Philip Brisbane (R-PA).

The man in the accompanying picture looked older than he had in the one Man of the People had sent me, but it was the same guy. I wasn't sure that I'd want to be called Flipper rather than Philip, or even Phil, but nicknames aren't always the result of personal preference. It was easy to see how Philip could morph into Flipper after a few keg-stands.

Dahlia must have seen a clip from the press conference on the news, and, as the official keeper of Gallagher's Ro-lodex, she must have known that Brisbane was in it and added things up on her own. She may even have scheduled meetings or conference calls for Gallagher, Brisbane, and Perry, although it would have been unwise of them to leave a public record of any tête-a-têtes outside of the occasional Princeton alumni event. Perhaps she'd even watched the Tiger deal unfold and recognized a similar pattern.

The article continued, nicely clearing up some other matters for me:

Senator Brisbane has been under intense pressure since Congressional Democrats launched an unexpected at-tack on his leadership last week, citing the unusual length of time the bill has spent in Committee as em-blematic of Republican foot-dragging.

The appropriations bill has important ramifications not only for the military but for the nation's defense industry. U.S. defense contractors, many of whom have been struggling in the current industrial climate, are eager to see this bill passed. Several of these compa-nies have been lobbying committee members aggres-sively.

The article went on to identify a number of companies by name and to discuss their lobbying efforts in greater detail. Thunderbolt Industries wasn't on the list, but it didn't have to be. There was no need for Thunderbolt to openly lobby the Senate Committee when its CEO went "way back" with the Committee's chairman.

Everything about the deal that hadn't made sense before now made complete sense. Thunderbolt's revenues were in decline and its current stock price was languishing because it had lost out on an important contract, one that Brisbane had used his position and influence to steer away from Thunderbolt in order to depress the company's performance. As a result, Perry could do his buyout at the depressed price, not to mention win concessions from the union. Then, once the appropriations bill passed, Brisbane could steer a few fat contracts Perry's way. Thunderbolt would flourish, and Perry could sell the company at a handsome profit, generating equally handsome returns for his investors. The previous shareholders would lose out, but I doubted Perry and his investors cared.

And I had a pretty good idea as to who some of those investors might be. I wasn't sure how they'd managed it—probably through an intricate tangle of trusts and front companies to mask their conflicts of interest—but it wouldn't surprise me one bit to learn that Flipper Brisbane and Glenn Gallagher both had considerable interests in the "investor group" backing Perry's management buyout.

Meanwhile, the accelerated schedule for getting the deal done was undoubtedly a direct result of the heightened pressure the esteemed senator was under to finalize the appropriations bill. Once the bill was approved, the ways in which Thunderbolt could benefit would cause the company's stock price to pop. If Perry didn't get the deal done before this happened, he and his investors would lose out.

The scope of both the planning and the duplicity was breathtaking, but they'd had practice, after all. I was sure that if I did a little more research, I'd find that the Tiger buyout had followed the same pattern.

And then I realized something else. If Jake had worked on the Tiger deal, he'd had a chance to see Gallagher, Perry, and Brisbane pull their first scam. While it was unlikely that Gallagher had confided in Jake, much less cut him in on either deal, Jake must have figured out that Gallagher and his cronies were attempting a repeat performance of their first success.

This time, however, Jake had also figured out a way to get a piece of the action. Because the investment had been made during Gallagher and Annabel's marriage, its proceeds would probably be fair game even under the most stringent of prenuptial agreements. If the investment generated the same sort of returns the Tiger investment had generated, it would mean enough money to set anyone up for life, even in the style to which Annabel was accustomed.

But neither Annabel nor Jake would be able to enjoy those proceeds if the deal didn't go as planned.

chapter twenty-seven

I'd found the key that unlocked the answers—or most of them, at least. But I still needed proof. And I needed it soon, ideally before Thunderbolt's shareholders agreed to sell their company at an artificially depressed price the next day.

I was so deep in thought that when Peter placed a hand on my shoulder, I gave a startled yelp. A librarian promptly shushed me from her post at the checkout desk, her glare disapproving behind thick glasses. I mouthed a sheepish apology, even as I wondered whether the glasses came with the job or were a prerequisite to getting it. She continued to glare at me for a long moment before returning to stamping whatever she was stamping.

"Read this," I whispered to Peter, tugging at his sleeve with one hand and pointing with the other to the *Washington Post* article on the screen before me.

He pulled up a chair and scrolled quickly through the article. It didn't take him long to put the pieces together. "Unbelievable. They had the entire thing rigged."

"But we still can't prove it."

"There's got to be a trail, somewhere. Something that will prove what Gallagher and Perry and Brisbane were all up to."

"They've probably covered their tracks pretty well. We really need someone on the inside, somebody at Thunderbolt who can help."

"Well, if we're lucky, Man of the People will be that somebody. Assuming we can figure out who he is. Which reminds me—I had an idea while I was on the phone. May I?" he asked, reaching out his hand for the mouse.

"Sure." He sent a copy of the *Washington Post* article to the printer and then returned to the search bar. I watched as he typed in "Man of the People" and "Thunderbolt."

"Oh. I should have thought of that." Two heads were definitely better than one, especially when that one was mine.

"It probably won't lead anywhere," he said, pressing enter. A long list of results filled the screen, but they were for sites about Greek and Norse gods interspersed with a few for evangelical groups. "At least, not anywhere useful. I had a feeling it was a long shot."

"But it was a good idea."

He shrugged. "Ready to get going?"

I nodded and reached for my jacket. He moved the mouse to close out of the search engine, but then he hesitated.

"Maybe I'll just try one more thing." He added "Industries" to "Thunderbolt" in the search bar, pecking at the letters with his index fingers. Peter's business revolved around computers, but he had never thought that sufficient reason to learn how to type.

I was expecting that the search engine would return with no results this time, instead of too many about things we didn't care about, but a short list appeared on the screen. They were all links to the Web site of a Pittsburgh newspaper.

"That's more like it," I said approvingly.

"Unless it's an exposé on Thor." Peter clicked on one of the links and an article popped up in the browser.

Union Threatens Walk Out at Thunderbolt
Talks continued into the early morning as Thunderbolt Industries management and union officials struggled to reach agreement. At stake are the terms for the new labor contract.
"Management is asking for cuts in health care and pension benefits for our hardworking members. Meanwhile, they reward themselves with big bonuses and fancy cars. I'm going to keep fighting until I have something that I can feel proud to present to our union members," said union chapter president Frank Kryzluk. "We're not going to just lie down and let the military-industrial complex steamroll right over us little guys."

"New union troubles?" I asked, momentarily confused. Then I checked the article's date—it had been posted weeks ago.

"No, just the same old union troubles, I guess."

"Well, we know how it ended. Perry and his executive

team extracted some concessions on benefits, but not as many as they'd hoped. The union held pretty firm. On Monday Perry said that they'd wrapped up negotiations over the weekend." I scanned the rest of the article. "I wonder why this even came up in the search results. There's no 'man of the people' reference in here." I pushed my chair back and stood to put on my coat.

I had collected the *Washington Post* article from the printer and was stashing it in my pocket when I heard Peter's shout.

"Aha!"

This time the librarian's shushing was even more emphatic, but when Peter gave her his own apologetic look, instead of continuing to glare at him she made a "don't-worry-about-it" face. I knew from experience that Peter's apologetic look was very convincing, but her easy capitulation seemed unfair. However, I had more important things to worry about than battling the librarian's double standard.

"Aha what?" I asked.

"Here." He pointed to the screen. A sidebar ran alongside the main article.

Pittsburgh's Own Michael Moore
Union president Frank Kryzluk was a local celebrity even before he assumed his prominent role in union affairs. His weekly talk show on public access television, *Frank Talk with Frank,* is a runaway hit with viewers and has earned him comparisons to activist filmmaker Michael Moore (although critics contend that Kryzluk, like Moore, occasionally lets conspiracy theories get the better of him).

As one fan explains, "Frank's just a regular guy, you know? A real man of the people—"

"Aha!" I cried.
This time even Peter couldn't soothe the librarian's ire.

It was nice to finally know who we were looking for. Unfortunately, while Frank Kryzluk may have been a regular guy and a real man of the people, his democratic leanings didn't extend to listing his number or address in the local phone book, nor could we find it on the Web. This was probably a wise precaution if he was as much of a local celebrity as the article claimed, but it was a bit frustrating for our purposes.

So we were back to our original plan, albeit with far more focus than we'd had initially. Now we had a name, and even a picture from the paper. It showed a shaggy-looking man in his fifties. His expression was good-humored beneath a trucker's cap.

"See," said Peter, pointing to the cap. "Everyone's wearing them."

I left him making amends to the librarian and returned to the pay phone to call Luisa.

"Didn't I just talk to you?"

"Yes, but I have a new assignment for you."

"Goody," she said dryly. "What do you want this time? Everything Oprah's worn in the past month? The personal challenges facing the guests on Dr. Phil? Or how about that Judge Judy person? Do you want me to investigate her?"

"Close. Sort of."

"You mean, you actually want me to do legal work?" she asked when I'd explained what I needed.

"You are a lawyer," I pointed out. "If anyone can connect Gallagher and Brisbane to Perry's investor group, it's you, right? There have to be legal records of front companies and partnerships and stuff like that."

"I guess it's better than watching more television."

Peter was surprisingly good at chatting up the librarian, and she turned out to be surprisingly useful once she got over the glaring thing.

"The Tick Tock Tavern," she told us with certainty. "That's where you want to go. They have a special on Fridays: two-dollar pitchers from five to seven. And it's practically across the street from the Thunderbolt plant. You can't miss it."

Because I had formally relinquished my navigating responsibilities to Peter, we didn't miss it. At exactly 5:00 p.m., we were standing in front of a low cinder-block building adorned with a neon sign welcoming us to the Ti k ock Tav rn. Another sign, which was either better cared for or more resilient, assured us that we would find Iron City beer on tap at this establishment.

"Ready?" asked Peter, settling his trucker's cap more firmly on his head.

"I hate that hat."

"Maybe it'll grow on you after you have a few brewskies." He pushed open the outer door.

"Brewskie?" I asked, following him inside.

The interior was dimly lit and furnished with the expected assortment of Formica tables with faux-wood finish and chairs upholstered in cracked and peeling vinyl. A man was perched on a stool behind the bar. He'd been reading but looked up as we approached.

"What can I get you folks?" he asked.

"Iron City?" suggested Peter, raising an eyebrow at me.

"Why not? With a Diet Coke chaser?"

The bartender closed his book and placed it on the rear counter next to the cash register. I made a mental bet—either *The DaVinci Code* or *The Illustrated DaVinci Code*—before stealing a glance at the title. It was Edith Wharton, *House of Mirth*.

"How are you liking Lily Bart?" I asked as the bartender poured our drinks. He glanced over from the tap in surprise. The economics half of my double major may have proved more lucrative over the years, but the literature half occasionally came in handy.

"She's something," he said, his tone admiring. "I just hope she ends up with that Selden guy."

Half an hour later, the bartender and I were debating Wharton's use of symbolism, we were on our second round of drinks, and the place was starting to fill up.

Half an hour after that, the bartender was our new best friend, we were on our third round of drinks, and the place was packed.

And a half hour after that, our new best friend was personally introducing us to Frank Kryzluk. Apparently, he'd managed to come in and seat himself in the back without us even noticing, probably at some point between rounds three and four.

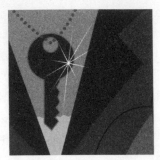

chapter twenty-eight

As far as I could tell, Peter and Frank Kryzluk had nothing in common beyond both being males of the human variety.

Peter was the son of a lawyer and a doctor and had been raised in an environment of enlightened liberalism, complete with whole-grain baked goods, organic vegetables, fervent recycling, and family vacations that involved hiking, cross-country skiing, and other healthy and ecofriendly pastimes. When he left his parents' comfortable Bay Area home, he didn't go far, earning his degree at Stanford and then returning promptly to San Francisco. In fact, before his recent move to New York, he'd never lived anywhere but northern California. He was handsome in a boy-next-door kind of way, and his quiet charm sometimes made it easy to forget just how smart he was. He also seemed to have been spared the gene that was responsible for interest in professional sports, golf, and cigars, and, until the advent

of the trucker cap, he had never dressed in a way that embarrassed me.

Frank Kryzluk had a couple of decades and more than a
couple of pounds on Peter, and he wore his flannel and re-
laxed-fit denim ensemble as if this was his customary attire.
He'd never attended college but had gone directly from high
school to his first factory job. "I got my union card the same
day I got my diploma," he told us proudly in a booming
voice, after insisting that we toast to the Steelers.

Given their differences in background and interests, I
could come up with only one explanation for why Peter and
Frank hit it off so well and so fast: the hats. Frank's trucker
cap was almost identical in style to Peter's, albeit more worn
and adorned with a Steelers logo. And, to my eye at least,
Frank's hat looked like it belonged on his head, whereas
Peter's didn't quite seem to fit.

But it was as if wearing the hat had changed more than
Peter's usual fashion statement. His voice was louder, and his
manner was practically gregarious. He was also exhibiting
a taste for draft beer—and belching—that was completely
unfamiliar to me and more than a little disconcerting. I
only liked to drink beer with spicy food, so after a few sips
and in the absence of a decent Pinot Grigio or Shiraz, I'd
focused my attentions on Diet Coke. Peter, however, had
been sucking down glass after glass of beer, and he didn't
stop when we joined Frank at his table. Watching the two
men bond over Iron Cities, I made an executive decision
that once it had fulfilled its current mission, Peter's favorite
new accessory was going to mysteriously disappear.

Kryzluk's initial reaction when we introduced ourselves was a mix of surprise, concern, embarrassment, and curiosity. Surprise because he thought he'd warned us off, concern because of the dangerous turn events had taken, embarrassment because he'd both enjoyed and recognized the absurdity of his cloak-and-dagger shenanigans, and curiosity because he was eager to hear if we'd turned up any new info.

"Why didn't you just tell me that you thought Perry had Brisbane manipulating the contracts?" I asked, trying not to sound impatient.

Frank rubbed his nose, which was on the large side and reddish in color. "I didn't have any way to know for sure. I had a hunch, but that was it. I was worried that you'd think I was some sort of crank, or not trust my motives, being the union president and whatnot. I thought I could give you some hints and get you interested. Then you'd start digging around."

"Why me?"

His nose grew redder. "Well, I don't know if you'll like the answer to this one."

"Try me."

"I had my daughter call that Gallagher guy's office and pretend she was Perry's secretary. She got a list of all the folks who were working on the buyout, and I thought you'd be the best person to contact, being a female and all. I wasn't trying to be a male chauvinist. It's just that sometimes women care more about these things." I had been a pretty soft touch as it turned out, so I probably couldn't blame him.

"Dahlia gave you my name, but how did you get my e-mail?"

"That was my daughter's doing, too." The pride in his voice was almost tangible. "She's only fourteen, but she's a real computer whiz. She figured that a young urban professional lady like yourself would probably have that fast Internet thing—"

"Broadband?" interjected Peter, popping a potato chip into his mouth. I brushed ineffectually at the crumbs that dropped on his sweater.

"Broadband, right. She figured out which companies offer that service where you live, and then she called them pretending to be you. After a couple of tries she found the right one. That's how she got your e-mail, and then she got me all set up to write to you. Wasn't that smart? She's a real pistol. She does all my research for my show, too. Did you know I'm a TV personality? *Frank Talk with Frank* it's called. Every Saturday morning on public access channel fifty-five."

It was a bit unsettling to learn that an adolescent girl in another state was successfully able to impersonate me and access my various service provider accounts, but I would worry about that later. Instead, with Peter's help, I brought Frank up to speed on our theory about Jake and Annabel being responsible for Gallagher's murder and the ways in which I had been set up to take the blame. "But not only do we not have any proof about what Perry and Brisbane and Gallagher were all up to, I'm wanted for murder and the real murderer and his girlfriend are about to make a mint."

"That's a real pickle," Frank agreed.

"My friend Luisa is checking for any sort of legal paper trail that can show that Brisbane and Gallagher were invested

in the deal, but I doubt she'll be able to find anything before the shareholder vote tomorrow morning."

"Well, I have a plan for that. I had to do something, and
I didn't realize you two were going to show up when you
did, so I hatched a plot of my own. But now that you're here,
I could sure use your help."

Frank told us his plan over more Iron City and in between
greeting the steady stream of "buddies" dropping by his
table to toast to the Steelers. He also insisted that we join
him in playing a few rounds of a game that involved trying
to throw miniature basketballs into miniature rings in order
to make different bells and buzzers go off. Apparently, the
bells and buzzers also indicated points accumulated. I wasn't
very good at this, but Peter was a natural. Frank was enthu-
siastic about his new protégé, and a great deal of high-
fiving, back-slapping and beer-glass-clinking ensued.

"Where are you kids staying tonight?" he asked. "Non-
sense," he said, when we told him we were going to find a
motel. "You'll stay with us. There's one of those pullout beds
in the rec room." He checked his watch. "But we should get
going. Little Frankie—that's my daughter—she's got her
band practice on Friday nights, but I like to be there when
she gets home."

I insisted on driving. I might be a little near-sighted, but
at least I wasn't drunk, and I wasn't sure I could say the same
for Peter. When all was said and done, Frank had probably
had two or three beers, and I was practically afloat on a sea
of Diet Coke, but Peter had gone through the better part

of a keg on his own. He boozily extolled Frank's virtues from the passenger seat as I concentrated on the taillights on Frank's battered minivan.

The Kryzluk residence was a modest ranch house on a street lined with similar houses. I parked Luisa's car at the curb as Frank pulled the minivan into the attached garage. Peter grabbed the small athletic bag that held our limited collection of belongings, and we followed our host inside.

For dinner, Frank had promised to whip up a batch of his homemade pierogies, which, according to him, were famous. Peter volunteered to help him out while I called in a quick update to Luisa. She had little new to report, except Hilary's frustration—apparently both Jake and the mysterious stranger had slipped her trail.

I'd finished the call and was trying to convince Peter and Frank that I could be sufficiently trusted with a knife to chop something when Frank's daughter arrived. From the way he'd spoken of Little Frankie, I'd automatically pictured a teenage-girl version of Frank in a polyester band uniform and befeathered hat lugging a tuba and a zip drive. Little Frankie, however, defied all expectations. She may have been a band member and computer whiz, but her fashion inspiration seemed to come from Gwen Stefani rather than Bill Gates, and she had more jewelry protruding from more piercings than I'd ever seen on one person's face.

Her behavior, however, was straight out of Emily Post. She greeted her father with affection and his guests with friendly welcome. When Frank suggested that she fetch clean linens and make up the bed in the rec room while he prepared dinner, she readily agreed. I offered to help, and she chattered on about her band and her blog as we carried sheets and blankets down into the basement.

The rec room appeared to serve many functions. A ping-pong table with a broken net was pushed up against a wet bar, and a classic Barbie town house sat on a cardboard box. "I had the same one," I said approvingly, pausing to admire it.

"I haven't played with it in years."

"Me, neither. But I really loved mine."

"Yeah, it's pretty cool." Frankie pulled on the string that moved the elevator up and down between the four stories. "I could probably sell it on eBay or something, but I'd rather hold on to it."

Camera cases and video equipment filled one corner, and green metal file cabinets filled another. Framed photographs vied for space on the crowded walls. "All of the family pictures are upstairs," explained Frankie. "These are just from my dad's other stuff—you know, the TV show, and union things."

I didn't recognize any of the people in the photos of Frank interviewing guests on a makeshift set, but I assumed that they were mostly area natives. There was a picture of a slightly younger Frank being sworn in as union chapter president, with a proud, younger, and less pierced Frankie at his side. Then there was a series of group photographs featuring men, women, and children decked out in red, white, and blue outfits.

"Those are from the annual union picnics," Frankie said, guiding me from photo to photo and narrating their progression. "This one's from forever ago; from before my dad was even president." A banner above the crowd indicated that the picture had been taken on the Fourth of July eight years earlier. I guessed that eight years qualified as forever when it accounted for more than half of your life. "See, there I am, and there's my dad."

I obediently followed her pointed finger with my eyes. Then I noticed the man next to Frank. "Who's that?" I asked. He looked both nondescript and somehow familiar.

"Him? That's Mr. Marcus—he was the union president before my dad—and that's his wife, Mrs. Marcus. She passed on, though. Cancer, I think. And these are their kids, Andrew and Bobby."

I looked at the first boy she pointed to, and then back at his father. "Andrew Marcus?"

"Yeah, that's him and Bobby. I haven't seen them in a couple of years, but they're a lot older than me anyhow. They both went off to college. I forget where they went, but they didn't move back here after. I mean, who'd want to, right? Especially after their mom died. I don't know where they live now, but it's got to be more interesting than Pittsburgh. Anything is."

"Andrew Marcus," I said again.

"Do you know him or something?" asked Frankie.

"Sort of," I said. Because I sort of did.

Just by a different name.

I may not have been able to see too well at a distance, but I could see just fine up close.

The boy smiling out from the picture was none other than a teenaged Mark Anders.

chapter twenty-nine

Frank related the sad saga of the Marcus family over a hearty meal of pierogies and yet more Iron City.

Our drive-through adventure was a distant memory by the time we sat down to dinner, and my Big Mac, however big, seemed like it had been eaten in another lifetime. But I'd still been wary when Frank had first heaped my plate with the Polish dumplings. I'd gotten over my concerns quickly. In fact, I was finding them surprisingly delicious. I made a mental note to ask Frank to teach Peter how to make them. Assuming Peter ever sobered up. While the beer had no discernible impact on our host, Peter's expression was taking on a glazed look. I had the unfortunate feeling that I was in for some world-class snoring later that night.

"Bill Marcus was a great guy," said Frank, stabbing a pie-rogie with his fork. "A real salt-of-the-earth type. We used to go to the games together." I didn't have to ask which games; it was clear even to me that he could only be refer-ring to football. "We'd go hunting together, too—me and him and his boys. Little Frankie here's a vegetarian. She never wants to go hunting with her old dad, do you, cupcake?"

"I'll go hunting with you when you go to Tai Chi with me," she told him mildly.

"Hunting?" Something clicked. I looked up from my plate. "They hunted?"

"Sure. Bill was a great shot. The kids, too."

"With rifles? Or with handguns?"

He snorted. "You ever try to bag a deer with a handgun? I'm talking rifles. What else would folks hunt with but a rifle or a shotgun? But if you're asking about handguns, sure—sometimes we'd go to the practice range and play around with those. Andrew really shined at it. He had crackerjack aim—even the instructors would stand around to watch."

"It must have been him." I poked Peter. "I'll bet you anything it was him."

He gave a start. "Ouch," he said, rubbing at his ribs.

"Mark, Andrew, whatever his name is. He must have been the other guy at the boat basin. He figured out what Jake was up to—maybe he overheard Jake on the phone with me that night, at the office—and then he followed him. And he managed to shoot the gun out of Jake's hand, in the dark, at a distance." I turned back to Frank. "Was Andrew Marcus that good a shot? Could he do something like that?"

"Probably. Andy won a bunch of contests they had at the range. He must have got it from Bill. Now, Bill—he was a truly great shot. And one of those natural leaders, too. They made him chapter president when he was just a young man. Usually nobody gets elected until they're in their late forties or early fifties, but Bill won by a landslide when he was only thirty-seven or thirty-eight."

"Why do you keep referring to him in the past tense?"

"Yeah, Dad. Why?" asked Frankie. "It's not like he's dead or anything. You stopped in to see him last week." Her various lip and tongue adornments didn't seem to be getting in the way of such mundane tasks as eating, although there was the occasional clinking noise as she chewed.

Frank shook his head and exhaled a slow breath. "Funny, I didn't even realize I was talking about him that way. He's changed a lot over the years."

"What happened?"

"Well, it's a long story, and not a happy one. I guess it all started back when Bill was the union president, right before the Tiger buyout. And he worked at Tiger, too. So before the deal was done, while Tiger was still in a slump, he was the one in charge of negotiating the labor contracts when they came up for renewal. And because Tiger was in such a slump, he wasn't exactly in a position of strength for the negotiating."

"And?" Peter prompted. *And* was a hard word to slur, and yet he managed to slur it. I reached out a hand to move his beer glass away from him, but it was already empty. Instead, I swiped his cap off his head and sat on it. His expression once he realized what I'd done was stunned, but the Iron City had slowed his reflexes and it was too late for him to act.

Frank was wrapped up in his story and didn't seem to notice. "Well, Bill had to make some difficult decisions, and he was in a real tight spot. Perry and his guys, they made him choose, and neither option was so good. He could either agree to layoffs, or he could agree to cutbacks in benefits. He chose the cutbacks. Better that people have jobs and incomes, right? I should know—Perry's got us in the exact same position now over at Thunderbolt. Right over the old barrel."

"So Marcus agreed to the cutbacks. Then what happened?"

"A couple of years later, Carol, his wife, got sick with cancer. I heard it was the sort of thing that usually has a decent survival rate. But I guess she wasn't having regular checkups—their health insurance didn't cover them anymore. When she finally got the diagnosis, she was pretty far gone. And then the HMO gave her a whole runaround, making it hard to see the right specialists and get the right treatment. I'm not saying that if she'd had decent health care coverage she wouldn't have died. I don't know that. But I do know that you want to feel like you've done everything possible when something like that happens." The way he said this made me wonder what had happened to Frankie's mother, but it seemed intrusive to ask. "Bill couldn't feel that way. If anything, he felt like it was all his fault."

"Because of the cutbacks he agreed to. The poor guy. It must have been terrible for him," said Peter. He was still slurring, but at least he seemed able to follow the conversation. And he looked much smarter without the cap, even though he had a bad case of hat head.

"Terrible doesn't begin to describe it. He was convinced

he'd failed everybody—his wife, his kids, the union—everybody. Meanwhile, Perry and his cronies took Tiger public again on the same day Carol Marcus died at three times the price they paid for it. They made out like bandits."

"Literally," I said.

Frank raised his bottle of Iron City to the light and squinted at it. "Bill always enjoyed a beer or two—most people do. But after Carol died, it wasn't just a beer or two. He started drinking, and drinking hard, and he's been doing it ever since. He resigned as union president, and eventually he lost his job at Tiger. He couldn't be counted on to show up, much less show up sober."

"Let that be a lesson to you," I muttered to Peter.

"Bill's been living all holed up like a hermit for years now. Won't hardly see anybody or talk to anybody. I think he collects some disability, and his kids send him some money, and his friends do what they can. Otherwise I don't know how he'd get by." Frank sighed again. "I drop in every so often to see him. In fact, he's the one that got me wondering when Perry started in on the Thunderbolt buyout. Bill's got boxes and boxes of articles on Perry, and Brisbane, and even on that Gallagher guy. He's the one who convinced me that there was something shady going on. It took awhile for me to take him seriously. Just between us, he's a bit off his rocker, and he's sort of obsessive on this topic."

"And one of his sons just happens to show up at my firm, eager to work with the banker who handled the Tiger deal. What do you think it means?" I asked. "It can't be a coincidence."

"Are you sure it's the same boy as in the picture?"

"Almost positive. The Mark Anders I know looks like an older version of that boy and a younger version of his father. Besides, the name is too similar for it not to be him. Andrew Marcus became Mark Anders."

"But why?"

"I wish I knew."

Peter leaned forward. "Maybe we're wrong. Maybe Jake didn't kill Gallagher. Maybe Mark—or Andrew, or whatever you want to call him—killed him."

"To avenge his mother's death in some way?" I thought about this. "It's possible, I guess, although there's a lot that it doesn't explain. Like why Jake then came after me. And Mark seems like such a mild-mannered guy."

"Andy was always a good kid," said Frank. "Responsible."

"Besides," I added, "if he were trying to avenge his mother by killing Gallagher, why would he attack Dahlia? What did she ever do to him? For that matter, why wouldn't he go after Perry? He's the most obvious target. Or even Brisbane?"

"It doesn't add up," Peter agreed. "But he must have something to hide. Why else would he change his name? And say he was from New Jersey when he's from here? And not mention that he knew Perry and his entire history?"

"Maybe he's just trying to distance himself from an unhappy past," offered Frankie. "By changing his name, he can be someone different. That's what people do online—they make up different names, and they can be whoever they want to be."

"Maybe," I said. "But he wasn't exactly distancing himself by following Gallagher to Winslow, Brown."

Dessert was chocolate pudding served in individual plastic containers. This, too, was surprisingly delicious. Even better, apparently I could buy it right off the shelf at my local grocery or deli. Or so Frank assured me when I asked him to include it in the cooking lesson he'd offered to give Peter.

It was close to eleven by the time we'd polished off dessert, tidied up the kitchen, and finished finalizing our plans for the following day. Peter and I retired to the basement rec room, where, his moment of lucidity clearly over, he pitched himself fully-dressed onto the sofa bed. Given the snoring that began the second he hit the bed, it was a good thing he was facedown—that way the noise was at least partially muffled by the pillows.

I slipped into the pajamas Frankie had loaned me—cozy pink flannel with a pattern of gray elephants—pushed at Peter until he only occupied two-thirds of the bed, and lay down beside him. Despite the activity of the day and the heavy meal, I realized that it wasn't going to be easy getting to sleep. I was wondered-out, at least temporarily, on the topic of Andrew Marcus/Mark Anders, but there were a number of other things that seemed likely to keep me awake.

My usual level of caffeine intake was sufficiently high that I was practically immune to its effects, but I had set a personal record in Diet Coke consumption that evening. There was also a small window set high in the wall, at ground level with the front of the house, allowing a sliver of yellow light to stream in from the street. Of course, the windows of my bedroom in New York let in far more ambient light, but this lone sliver was somehow more distracting than what filtered into my apartment. And then there was Peter's snoring. In Manhattan, there were sirens and traffic noises and the occasional shout ricocheting up from the pavement. It was loud, but to me it was soothing, analogous to one of those sound machines featured in *SkyMall Magazine* along with the electrodes that promised to reshape even the flabbiest abs into a six-pack. Here the surrounding silence threw the snoring into high relief.

I flipped onto my stomach, but this didn't make me any more sleepy. I began counting sheep, but that made me think about wool, which made me wonder if I should learn how to knit, which reminded me of a particularly unpleasant elementary school crafts project involving yarn and sticks. Soon I caught myself mentally giving my former art teacher a piece of my mind, which left me more revved up than I had been before I started with the sheep.

I flipped back onto my back. Maybe it would help if I could get Peter to stop snoring.

I tapped him gently on the shoulder. "Stop snoring," I said politely.

He grunted and continued to snore.

I tapped him again, harder, and repeated my request, albeit less politely.

This time he didn't even grunt, but the snoring continued.

I had resorted to a childhood game—picking shapes out of the shadows the light cast on the opposite wall—when I realized that not only were the shadows moving, the light was changing color. Red and blue alternated with the yellow.

I heard footsteps, and then the lights were temporarily blocked out by moving figures on the front walk.

I sat up in bed.

It looked like we had company.

And it was the sort that came accompanied by flashing red–and–blue lights.

chapter thirty

I probably should have panicked, but I was getting a bit jaded. The entire fugitive-from-justice thing was losing what limited novelty value it had once had.

I sighed, pulled my sweater on over Frankie's pajamas, and stuffed my bare feet into my shoes. It took a few concerted shoves to rouse Peter from his Iron City-induced coma, but once up he moved quickly. In our haste, he forgot about his cap. I didn't, however. Under the cover of darkness, I slipped it discreetly into the folds of the sofa bed as we trundled it back up.

There was a glint of light on metal on the stairway, and I gasped. Perhaps I was more scared than I realized.

But it was only Frankie. "Follow me," she whispered, seemingly unaware of the way in which the red and blue of the police flashers bounced off the jewelry studding her face.

At least I had one question answered: apparently she did not remove the various rings and studs when she went to sleep.

There were heavy footsteps above us and the sound of Frank's booming voice. "What car?" he was asking. "Oh, the one parked on the street? It's not mine, but I sure wish it was." Even from a distance his tone sounded forced; I might have finally found someone who lied even less well than I did.

I hoped that the car had attracted interest simply because of the make, model, and location and not because they'd somehow connected its plates to Luisa and then to me. But then I heard another voice and the phrase "murder suspect." It looked like we were going to have to abandon Luisa's car for the time being.

Frankie guided us quickly through an adjacent utility room where a clothesline caught Peter square in the throat.

"Ooof," he wheezed, belatedly ducking his head.

The bolt on the cellar door groaned as Frankie undid it, and the squeal of the hinges sounded like an airhorn in the still night. A dog barked in the yard next door.

"Come on," Frankie urged under her breath as we climbed a set of concrete stairs. And then she took off across the grass.

Frank hadn't mentioned anything about Frankie being the star of her school track team, but maybe he had been too busy talking up her computer skills. I ran after her at a sprint, and Peter brought up the rear. We reached a chain-link fence, which Frankie scaled with practiced ease. Peter hoisted me up before clambering over it himself.

We were now in the yard of the home directly behind Frank's. "This way," whispered Frankie, hanging a sharp left.

Her pace didn't slow as we scrambled after her, across one yard and then another, skirting the occasional above-ground pool and tarpaulin-covered grill and leaving a trail of barking and yipping dogs in our wake. I caught a brief glimpse of a white poodle throwing itself against a picture window in an agitated frenzy, frustrated by its inability to give chase as we ran past.

Each backyard gave way to a new one in a seemingly endless chain, and my breath was ragged by the time we vaulted a final hedge and hit sidewalk. Frankie drew up short, and I nearly collided with her.

"Where are we going?" Peter asked, skidding to a stop behind me. I was breathing too hard to talk. I'd forgotten just how much I hated suburbia.

"Get down!" said Frankie, yanking my arm. We dived back behind the hedge we'd just vaulted. A second later a police cruiser glided slowly by. Through the leaves, I could make out the faces of the men inside, carefully surveying the quiet street. I willed the car to pass.

Instead, the car drew to a full stop. The night was so quiet that I could hear the sound of a window being lowered. Suddenly, a bright spear of light pierced the ground in front of me.

I held my breath, and I could sense Peter and Frankie holding theirs, too, as the officer panned the flashlight beam over the hedge and assorted other flora lining the sidewalk.

Only a few seconds must have passed, but it felt like hours

before the beam was shut off. I could hear the window being raised again, and the car's tires rolling down the street.

We breathed a collective sigh of relief and picked ourselves up from the ground, brushing at the leaves and twigs clinging to our clothing.

Then there was a sudden click, and a blinding light.

"Where do you think you're going?" a strange voice asked.

I was at a loss for words.

So I screamed instead.

chapter thirty-one

It was an impressive scream—I'd been getting a lot of practice, after all—but it was met with a cackle of laughter.

Frankie put her hands on her hips.

"Not funny," she said emphatically.

"It's sort of funny," replied the strange voice.

"Put that flashlight out," Frankie said. "Now, Aunt Wanda. Before the cops come back."

"I'm not the one waking up the neighborhood. Does your friend think she's auditioning for one of those horror movies?" But she switched off the light. "So, you folks going to come inside, or are you planning on hanging out in the bushes and yelping all night?"

It was convenient that Frank's sister, Wanda, lived within sprinting distance, and it was fortunate that she was an insomniac. She welcomed the wee-hour excitement of our arrival even if she was disappointed when nobody wanted to while away what remained of the night in a game of canasta.

"What's canasta?" Peter asked in a low voice as we trailed Wanda and Frankie up the stairs.

We were ushered into a room that belonged to Wanda's daughter, Diana, now away at college. "Just make yourselves right at home," she told us. "Frankie here can bunk down on the couch in the den. You kids sleep well." She shut the door behind her, but we could still hear her trying to entice Frankie into a game of cards as they moved down the hallway.

I was concerned that I wouldn't be able to sleep at all, let alone well, with so many posters of Justin Timberlake staring down at me, but it turned out that our mini-marathon proved to be an excellent cure both for my own insomnia and for Peter's snoring. We awakened to sunlight streaming in through the lace-curtained windows and the delicious smell of frying bacon wafting up from the kitchen.

Wanda provided us with fresh disguises (a Steelers baseball cap for Peter and sunglasses and a headscarf printed with an image of Princess Diana for me) and a breakfast that included not only bacon, but pancakes, eggs, sausage, fried potatoes, and sticky buns, all elegantly presented on Princess Diana memorial dishes. After breakfast, we climbed into Wanda's minivan for the ride to Thunderbolt headquarters. Peter and I hunched down in the back while she waved a stock certificate at the guard manning the security booth. The lot was so filled with cars and people that we felt safe once we passed through the gates, blending in easily with the crowd.

I was in high spirits, excited to see how events would play

themselves out that morning, but Peter was grumpy. He seemed unable to fully open his eyes, and the whites that were visible were more red than white. If I were a nicer person, I would have been more sensitive to his condition, especially since I was usually the one suffering the morning-after effects of immoderate drinking. But the very rarity of Peter's hangover made it too good an opportunity to resist.

"I'm not hung over," he insisted. "Just tired."

"Are you sure you didn't have one too many Iron Cit—"

"Don't say it."

"Say what?"

"You know."

"You mean, Iron Cit—"

"You did it again."

"This is a fun game."

He growled.

We joined the men and women filing through an entrance that was most definitely not on the glass-annexed executive side of the building. The wide concrete-floored hallway led us into a large room filled with rows of collapsible metal chairs. Judging by the framed notices on the walls, a number of which provided instructions regarding steps to take in the event of a choking, I guessed this was the employee lunchroom, temporarily pressed into service for the shareholder meeting. A makeshift dais with a podium had been erected at the far end.

The seats were already filling up, but there was a knot of

people clustered off to one side, and I could see the top of a familiar trucker's cap at the center of the group. Frankie and Wanda went to join Frank while Peter and I found empty chairs off the aisle in a row near the back.

We watched as a man mounted the dais to test the podium microphone. He kneeled and fiddled with some wires, and the microphone screeched to life, causing at least half the crowd to jump. Next to me, Peter moaned and clutched at his head.

A side door opened, and a line of suited executive types streamed through, climbing the steps to the dais and arranging themselves on the chairs that faced out onto the audience. The man at the microphone tapped it with his finger, which made it screech some more. Satisfied, he relinquished his post to one of the new arrivals, who cleared his throat and urged people to take their seats. The hum of conversation died down as the crowd sat, and soon every chair was filled, although there were still people standing against the walls. Most of the audience looked like Thunderbolt employees, but here and there I spotted more Yuppie-ish individuals who likely represented institutional shareholders.

The new man at the podium mumbled something about welcoming us all here today, being the secretary of Thunderbolt's board of directors, and calling the meeting to order before introducing Thunderbolt's chairman and CEO.

I squinted up at the dais. "Is that Jake?" I asked Peter in a whisper. "Two over from the right?"

"Rachel. That's a woman. She's wearing a skirt. And she has gray hair. She looks nothing like Jake."

"Oh. I knew that. I just wanted to see if you knew that, too."

"Jake's the third one in on the left."

"Still up for beating him silly after the meeting? Or are you too 'tired'? Maybe you'd rather just go out for a couple of Iron Cit—"

"Don't." His expression was pained.

A tall dark-suited man stepped up to the podium. He was too far away for me to make out his features, but fortunately the previous speaker had already introduced him as Nicholas Perry. And I would have recognized his oily voice from when we'd met on Monday. A lot had happened since then.

"Good morning," Perry said. "And thank you all for coming today." He added a few more words of welcome before getting to the point. "You've been invited here today to vote on a proposed sale of the company to a group of private investors led by myself. The board has discussed this matter at great length, and we feel it is the best way to maximize value for you, our shareholders. However, we've asked our financial advisor, Jake Channing of Winslow, Brown, to join us. Mr. Channing will provide you with an overview of the proposed buy—"

"Nick!" Frank yelled from the midst of his posse, which was clustered against one of the walls about halfway down the room. "Hey, Nicky! Over here!" The knot of people shifted, and one of them hoisted up a bright light while two others raised large cameras to their shoulders. One camera focused on Perry while the other focused on Frank.

Perry shielded his eyes against the light. "Who is that? We'll be doing a question-and-answer session aft—"

"It's Frank Kryzluk, Nick, a shareholder and president of your local union chapter. Remember me from those contract negotiations? Good times, right? You might not know that I also host a TV show in my spare time. *Frank Talk with Frank,* on public access channel fifty-five. Today we're broadcasting live right here from the Thunderbolt shareholders' meeting. Isn't that something?"

"Well, Frank, I don't know if that's the sort of thing that's generally done at shareholders' meetings," Perry said smoothly, but not before shooting the security guards nearest him a pointed look. They just shrugged. Perhaps they were members of the union, too.

"Well, Nick, maybe we should vote on it." Frank turned to the crowd. "All those in favor, say 'aye.'"

He was rewarded with a boisterous chorus of "ayes" as the cameramen panned the room.

"I guess that's settled, then. And who's in favor of starting the question-and-answer session right now?"

He was rewarded with another, even more boisterous chorus of "ayes," and it seemed as if the entire audience raised their hands at once. Frank had prepped his friends well. I'd known what was coming, but I was still finding the performance highly enjoyable.

Perry gazed out at the sea of hands, but before he could call on anyone, a voice rang out from a rear row. "Hey, Nick, you made a bundle on the Tiger deal, didn't you? Are any of the same investors involved in this buyout?"

"Uh—" Perry began.

"What happened at Tiger, Nick?" yelled somebody else from a row in the front and on the right. "You couldn't get any government contracts when the public owned the company, but when you owned the company, the contracts came flooding in. Why was that, Nick?"

"Are you counting on being able to get government contracts after you do the Thunderbolt buyout, Nick?" This came from halfway down on the left.

"Yeah, Nick. What's going on? Do you have the entire Armed Forces Committee in your pocket?"

"Or just Senator Brisbane?"

"Didn't you two go to college together?"

The questions were coming from every direction, at a rapid clip and in a carefully rehearsed sequence. Perry couldn't get a word in, but I really wished I could make out the expression on his face.

"Is your old friend Flipper Brisbane sitting on the Appropriations bill until after the buyout?"

"So you can do the buyout for peanuts?"

"And then he'll steer some nice fat contracts your way?"

"Is that legal?"

"Yeah, Nick. Is it legal to fix things up that way with your buddy Flipper?" This last was from Frank, who'd moved forward so that he was standing only a few feet from the stage.

Perry sputtered and looked behind him for support. Jake, that prince among men, didn't seem to be rushing to his aid, nor did any of the board members.

Then a new voice rang out from the back. "And what happens to the workers, Nick? Do you care about them?"

This was unplanned, and the speaker's voice held such emotion that I spun around to see who it was. Even though I already thought I knew.

Mark Anders, or, more accurately, Andrew Marcus, was standing at the top of the aisle, his face white and drawn, his jaw set, and his hands stuffed in his pockets.

"Do you care if their benefits get cut, or if they can't pay their medical bills?" he demanded, advancing down the aisle with measured steps. Only a slight crack in his voice betrayed any nervousness.

"Do you care?" he repeated. "Do you care?"

Suddenly, it was if time downshifted into low gear, and the noise of the crowd receded. Andrew's right arm appeared to move in slow motion as he began pulling something from the pocket of his windbreaker.

One face in the blur of people behind Andrew swam into focus. Even without the deep bruise, I would have recognized the mysterious dark-haired stranger. Our eyes met, and we rushed forward at the same moment.

"Nooooooooooo!" I cried, lunging for Andrew's gun arm as the shots rang out.

chapter thirty-two

We hit the floor in a tangle: Andrew, the mysterious stranger, and me.

My fingers scrambled for purchase on the slippery nylon of Andrew's windbreaker. "Stop," I pleaded. "You don't want to do this."

"I have to do this," he said between clenched teeth. "And I don't want to hurt you, so let go."

He shook me off and raised his arm, pointing the gun toward the dais again.

Then I saw the mysterious stranger's hand descend, chopping fiercely at Andrew's wrist. He gave a shout of pain and dropped the gun. I kicked at it, sending it spinning down the cold concrete floor.

Andrew struggled to his feet, intent on recovering the weapon. The stranger and I both leaped to tackle him, but he was too fast. My arms closed around empty air, and I hit the floor again, but this time the stranger cushioned my impact.

The audience finally started to react. Somebody grabbed Andrew's gun, and a couple of people grabbed Andrew.

On the dais, the board of directors began cautiously emerging from the chairs they'd dived behind, and Perry pulled himself up from where he'd ducked behind the podium. He was clutching at his arm. It was a good thing that I couldn't see that well, as I had a feeling there was blood involved, and I'd gotten more than my fill of gore seeing to the mysterious stranger's cut the night before last.

"Are you okay up there?" asked the mysterious stranger. His voice was surprisingly deep.

"What? Oh. Sorry." I rolled off him.

Wordlessly, he helped me up before melting into the crowd.

Andrew was confessing to Gallagher's murder even as the authorities led him away, assuring them and everyone else within earshot that he wouldn't rest until Perry and Brisbane were also six feet under. We found out later that his brother, Bobby, had made a similar attempt on the good senator's life that very morning, intercepting Brisbane outside of his Washington home. An off-duty Secret Service agent on his morning run had jogged by at just the right time— at least, the right time for Brisbane. Otherwise, the brothers would have been two for three.

Their original plot had been much more elaborate than what eventually played out, the product of more than a year of careful planning. Just as Andrew had insinuated himself into Gallagher's workplace, Bobby had recently secured an internship in Senator Brisbane's office. They intended to make their respective employers' deaths look like accidents before moving on to Perry.

But once Perry launched the Thunderbolt buyout, they had to scrap their careful plans. They couldn't let Perry and his cronies do to other families what had been done to theirs. They were willing to sacrifice their futures to avenge their mother's death, but there were three targets, and only two of them. They had to kill one of the men on their list without being caught so that they could remain free long enough to finish the job.

They were fortunate in that there was a long line of people who wanted to kill Gallagher, and Andrew improvised a murder that could have been committed by a number of them. This left the brothers free to kill Brisbane and Perry in parallel, at which point they would confess to the Gallagher murder, as well.

The irony, of course, was that their only successful murder was the one for which they didn't want to be caught. Killing people should have been a lot easier when they weren't concerned about the consequences.

Peter and I spent the rest of the morning and a significant chunk of the early afternoon making statements to the police. They seemed willing to suspend my fugitive status now they had the real killer in custody, and by midafternoon we'd said goodbye to the extended Kryzluk family and were back in Luisa's car, heading east on the Interstate.

This time Peter knew better than to order a salad at the McDonald's drive-through.

Traffic was light, and the weather was clear, so the drive back was pleasant and relatively quick. We'd called from the road to update my friends, and they were waiting for us in my apartment. They'd also already ordered dinner.

Over the past several days I'd eaten Big Macs, pierogies, bacon, sausage, pancakes, coffee cake, various forms of fried potatoes (including several bags of salt-and-vinegar chips), enchiladas, guacamole, pad thai, spring rolls, and lasagna. At this point a normal person would probably be craving vegetables, or at least liposuction.

Fortunately, I wasn't normal, and I'd squeezed in a number of unintended workouts escaping from the police and assorted other pursuers. Otherwise I wouldn't have been able to do justice to the samosas and curry that arrived shortly after Peter and me.

"Anybody want a beer?" Hilary called out from the kitchen.

"You told her to say that," Peter accused me.

I gave him my sweetest and most innocent smile.

We all took our plates into the living room, where Peter and I recounted everything that had happened since we'd last checked in.

"Was it like *The Bodyguard,* only you were Kevin Costner and Perry was Whitney Houston?" asked Hilary.

"And what is a pierogie, exactly?" asked Jane. She'd never lived anywhere but Boston, and her exposure to Eastern European cuisine had been limited, although she could probably discourse at length on clam chowder and baked beans.

"There's something I don't get," said Emma after the topics of Kevin Costner and pierogies had been thoroughly exhausted. "Why would Andrew attack Dahlia?"

I turned to her. "That's exactly what Peter and I were wondering. And we don't think he did. I mean, Andrew's small enough that he could pass for me if he was dressed in the right outfit, so he probably *could* have done it, but that doesn't explain why he would do it in the first place, much less why he would try to frame me. Meanwhile, the police seem ready to blame him, given that they let me completely off the hook."

"This Andrew person and his brother—their actions were fairly principled," mused Luisa. "In a somewhat twisted way, but still principled. Some might even find their reason for killing Gallagher honorable given the context. But that wouldn't extend to killing Dahlia, would it?"

"Even if it did, it still doesn't add up," said Peter. "Why would Andrew care if Dahlia had realized something fishy was going on with the Thunderbolt deal? If anything, he would have welcomed it. But how could he even know what Dahlia suspected?"

"Which brings us back to Jake and Annabel," I said. "Which also brings us back to the fact that Jake tried to shoot me at the boat basin."

"Rach, you're practically blind," Hilary said. "Are you absolutely sure Jake was shooting at you?"

"And if you're practically blind, why did you assure me that you were fine to drive my car?" added Luisa pointedly.

"It was Jake at the boat basin. I'm sure of that. And it was Mark—I mean, Andrew—who rescued me from him. There's only one possible explanation. Jake and Annabel may not have killed Gallagher, but that doesn't mean they didn't jump at the opportunity to make the most out of his death." I explained my theory about the likely terms of Annabel's prenuptial agreement. "The Thunderbolt deal had to go forward, at least if the two of them wanted to make sure they would have sufficient ill-gotten gains on which to live happily ever after. They wouldn't want to have to work for the rest of their lives, would they?"

"Did you tell the police about this?" asked Jane.

I shook my head. "I tried, but as far as they were concerned, they had a confessed killer and his brother on the hook. They weren't terribly interested in my theories."

The phone rang just then—not my BlackBerry, which I'd long since given up any hope of recovering from the tourist's backpack—but my home phone.

"Should I get that?" asked Peter. He consulted the caller ID on the handset. "It says Private Caller."

"Why don't we let the machine get it? Everyone I'd want to talk to is already here."

"How sweet," said Hilary dryly.

We could hear the answering machine from the study, and my voice inviting callers to leave a message. Then we could hear the caller leaving his message.

"Rachel, Jake here."

His tone was friendly. Like it never would have occurred to him to frame me for murder, much less try to kill me.

"Speak of the devil," said Jane.

"It's been a crazy couple of days, hasn't it? I still can't get over the news about Mark Anders. I heard that it was you who managed to get the gun away from him at the shareholders' meeting—nice work! I didn't even recognize you, and then I guess I missed you after. It was quite a scene. Give me a call when you get a chance. I want to make sure you're okay."

"The nerve of that guy!" said Peter. This was rapidly becoming his standard response to all matters involving Jake.

"He doesn't know that we know what we know," I told him. "But he probably wants to find out if we do know what we know, so that he can know if he needs to worry about what we know."

"When you put it like that, I don't know if *we* know what we know," said Luisa. She had opened both the window and the screen and was now perched on the sill, the hand with her cigarette held carefully outside.

"Luisa, you're making me very nervous," Jane said. "We're fifteen flights up."

"Actually, only fourteen. There's no thirteenth floor," I said.

Luisa just shrugged and exhaled a stream of smoke into the air above 79th Street.

"How do children in New York learn to count, anyhow?" asked Jane.

"While we're on the subject of what we know, or don't know, or wherever we were, what about the mysterious stranger in the suede jacket?" asked Emma.

"That's right," said Hilary. "What about Mr. Mysterious? Who is he?"

"And why does he keep showing up everywhere and then disappearing again?" asked Jane.

The intercom chose that moment to buzz.

"That had better not be Jake," said Peter.

I got up and went to answer it.

"Miss Rachel?" said the doorman. I'd long since given up on trying to convince him to drop the "miss."

"Yes?"

"There's a man here to see you? He said you'd recognize him from his black eye?"

"Speak of the other devil," I said.

"What's that?"

"Send him up, please."

chapter thirty-three

There were only four apartments on my floor, but their front doors opened onto a space so small that it felt full when just one of my neighbors and I chanced to be in it at the same time. This didn't stop all six of us from rushing out to meet the mysterious stranger. We watched with great anticipation as the old-fashioned dial above the elevator began to trace its slow path from the lobby up to fifteen.

The elevator dial stopped for a long moment at three. "One would think that a person could walk up two flights of stairs," said Luisa.

"That was probably Mr. and Mrs. Ditweiler. He has a touch of rheumatism in his knee, and she just had her hip replaced a few months ago," I explained. "She makes gingerbread men for the building Christmas party every year. They're really good."

The dial resumed its path, creeping along to five, six and seven. Then it stopped again at eight.

"The mysterious stranger is big on building suspense, isn't he?" said Hilary.

"It's part of the whole mysterious thing," Emma told her.

"How much of their lives do you think New Yorkers waste waiting for elevators?" asked Peter.

"Less than Californians waste sitting in cars," I said.

The dial started moving again, this time advancing steadily onward from eight to twelve and then directly to fourteen.

"The poor kids," said Jane. "They have no reason to think that thirteen even exists."

The doors finally slid open, and the mysterious stranger stepped out, black eye and all.

"Hi!" cried Hilary. "I'm Hilary. Who are you?"

He looked from one face to another. I guessed he wasn't expecting to find such a crowd waiting for him. I cleared my throat and gave a little wave, and his gaze landed on me.

"Ms. Benjamin?"

"Why don't we skip right to first names?" I suggested. After all, we'd been spending a lot of quality time together of late.

"I'm Special Agent Lattimer. Ben Lattimer."

It was nice finally to have a real name for the guy— "Mysterious Dark-Haired Stranger in the Suede Jacket" had been more than a little cumbersome. But Ben didn't look anything like a special agent. He wasn't wearing a dark suit, white shirt, narrow tie, and sunglasses. Instead, he had on a pair of faded Levi's, a striped button-down, and, of course, his suede jacket.

"When you say Special Agent, what exactly are you a special agent of? Could we see some identification?" Peter asked, placing his hand on my shoulder. Only if you knew him as well as I did would you have picked up on the note of tension in his voice. He'd been both embarrassed and annoyed that a complete stranger had been in on the Andrew Marcus tackle with me. He'd also been less than appreciative when I pointed out that his Iron City consumption the previous evening might have slowed his reflexes.

Ben reached into his jacket and withdrew one of those leather badge holders you see on TV. He flipped it open. "FBI Financial Fraud Unit."

"Cool," said Hilary.

We all took turns studying Ben's ID before agreeing that it looked authentic and ushering him into the apartment. None of us was sure if it was appropriate to offer food to special agents, but it seemed rude to continue eating without making the offer, and he accepted with an enthusiasm that suggested he hadn't been recently feasting on pierogies, coffee cake, or Quarter Pounders with Cheese.

"I first got interested when Perry did the Tiger buyout," he told us between mouthfuls of curry. "Bill Marcus wrote us—the Unit, I mean—a bunch of letters outlining his theory."

"You pay attention to that sort of thing?" I asked in surprise. I didn't want to think about how much trouble I could have saved myself, not to mention everyone else in the room, if I'd simply reported my concerns to somebody like Ben in the first place.

"We get a lot of letters from crackpots," Ben acknowledged. "But you never know when one of those crackpots is going to be blowing the whistle on the next Enron."

"There seem to be a lot of crackpots in Texas," said Hilary. Ben looked at her blankly. "You know. Enron. Texas. Crackpots."

"Anyhow," continued Ben, "the Marcus letters were actually pretty coherent, at least compared to some of what we see. And the basic chronology and the people involved were exactly as Marcus outlined. Which made me think that maybe he wasn't your garden-variety crackpot. I started looking for a money trail, and it turned out that all three of the principals—Perry, Gallagher, and Brisbane—had some interesting offshore accounts."

"Were the accounts in their own names?" said Luisa. "Because I couldn't find a thing."

"Far from it. I'd heard that Gallagher was an expert at making money, but he was also an expert at hiding it. They were buried deep, hidden inside a maze of shell companies and private partnerships. It was a real mess, but once I located the accounts, I could begin tracing the flows of cash in and out."

"And then?" prompted Emma. "What happened then?"

Ben ran a hand through his dark hair. "And then a new

case came in, a live one, and I had to put the Tiger investigation on hold. After all, it was only a speculative thing, a routine follow-up on a letter from the crackpot file."

"But you kept with it anyway, right?" asked Jane, a firm believer in perseverance as a virtue.

"I'd hoped to keep with it in my spare time, but the new case didn't leave me with any. When it eventually wrapped, I wanted to go back to investigating the Tiger deal, but I was told that another agent had taken up where I left off and concluded there wasn't anything to it."

"Seriously?" I said. "Wow, those guys were good. I mean, if trained professionals couldn't find evidence of anything wrong—"

"Not so fast," said Ben. "That's not the whole story. I didn't think much about it at the time, and before long I was neck-deep in another new case, and then another, and after a while I'd pretty much forgotten about the Tiger deal. Until last week, that is. Which is when I read an article about the Thunderbolt buyout—"

"—which got you wondering," interrupted Hilary.

"Exactly. So I went to pull the Tiger file. Only—"

"—there was no Tiger file!"

"Hilary," Luisa said. "Let the man finish his own sentences."

"She's right, though, isn't she? The Tiger file was gone?" I asked.

"It was more than gone. There was no trace that it or even the letters from Bill Marcus had ever existed. Everything had been completely wiped from the system."

"That sounds like the sort of thing that happens in South

American dictatorships, where the government 'disappears' people," said Hilary.

"Thank you for perpetuating tired stereotypes of my homeland," said Luisa.

"Look," said Ben, "I don't know who erased the records, or where the order to do so came from, but remember a United States senator was involved. My initial investigation probably tripped an alarm or two somewhere important."

"Whatever happened to checks and balances?" asked Jane.

Ben shrugged. "The very fact that the records were gone confirmed for me that I'd been on to something. And the good news is, based on what we saw at today's shareholders' meeting, a lot of people suspected what Perry had going with Gallagher and Brisbane. With all of the shareholders present and the media coverage, there's no way there won't be a thorough investigation now. Perry and Brisbane may have dodged some very real bullets, but I think their respective careers may be over."

"But what about Jake Channing's career? You must have suspected him, too," Peter asked. "Or why else were you following him?"

"That's why I'm here," he said.

"Oh." I said knowingly. Then I realized I had no idea what he meant. "What do you mean 'that's why you're here'?"

"When I read about the Thunderbolt deal, and after finding the Tiger file gone, I decided it was worth looking into things on my own. I called Winslow, Brown on Monday morning pretending to be from Perry's office to get the names of the bankers working on the deal with Gallagher. I thought his team would either be in on the entire thing or would make good witnesses. Once I had your names, I did some digging. It didn't take long to find out that not only had Jake worked at Gallagher's old firm, he used to date Gallagher's wife, so I was suspicious of him from the beginning, and even more so once Gallagher was murdered."

"If you were investigating us, didn't you find out about Mark Anders actually being Andrew Marcus?" I asked. "Didn't that raise any flags or trip any alarms or anything?"

He shook his head. "No. It was sloppy of me, especially in retrospect, but I figured that looking into the junior associate would be a waste of time; he was unlikely to know much of anything. Instead I focused on Jake and on you, Rachel. I had my concerns about Jake, but you checked out clean. I wanted to approach you, but I wasn't sure how. I needed to get a better sense of whether I could trust you."

"And that's why you were eavesdropping when we were at the St. Regis on Tuesday night?" I asked.

He nodded. "Yeah. Sorry about that, but I didn't want to just march right up and introduce myself. Then Dahlia was attacked on Wednesday morning, and you disappeared, so I was left with Jake. I was trying to figure out my next move when I saw him meet up with Annabel Gallagher late on Wednesday."

"And you were following him on Thursday, when I saw you at Starbucks," I said.

"That's right. It didn't take long to put two and two together. I figured that they were behind both Gallagher's murder and the attack on Dahlia Crenshaw. In fact, I almost stopped you that afternoon, to try to warn you, but I was worried that you'd alert Jake, since you and he seemed to be friends, and I didn't want to lose track of him. That was an excellent disguise, by the way. I would never have recognized you if I hadn't been able to hear you and Jake talking."

"So you were following Jake. And you followed him to the boat basin on Thursday night."

"Not that I did much good there. I wasn't far behind him when I saw somebody else following him. Now I know it was Andrew Marcus, but at the time I thought it might have been another accomplice, so I had to give Jake more of a lead than I would have liked. And I didn't realize he was counting on meeting you there. Then I heard shots, and I came running—"

"—and collided into me," I concluded for him. "Sorry about that."

He gave me a sheepish smile. "Occupational hazard."

"Okay. So you were on to Jake and Annabel. But what do you want from us?" asked Peter.

"I'm on to Jake and Annabel—it sounds like we're all on to Jake and Annabel—but we don't have any proof."

"Jake seems to think he can bluff his way though," I told Ben, explaining about the e-mail Jake had sent me and his message from earlier that night. "And he thinks I'm clueless enough to buy his bluff."

"The nerve of that guy," Peter muttered.

"Good," said Ben. "Then I think we have a chance."

chapter thirty-four

Sunday morning felt like spring, as if March had skipped over April and gone straight to May. A gentle breeze wafted a strand of hair across my face as I got out of the cab. After several rigorous shampooings, my hair was back to its original dark red, and while I'd declared the results of my adventures in alternative hair color inconclusive—the Madonna wig left me with sincere doubts as to just how much more fun blondes had, and my experience as a brunette had been too action-packed to offer a valid basis for comparison—it was nice to once again recognize my image in mirrors and other reflective surfaces.

The streets of Chinatown were thronged with honking cars, and the sidewalks were thronged with pedestrians. I wondered who had decreed that dim sum was a good idea for brunch. I was as fond of dumplings as the next person, but to me brunch just wasn't brunch without Hollandaise and hash browns. Still, when Jake had suggested dim sum it seemed appropriate to feign enthusiasm, so here I was at the corner of Bowery and Canal Street, trying my best to ignore the animal carcasses hanging in the shop windows. As a general rule, the less my food resembled actual living beings the more appealing I found it.

"Stop rubbing your ear like that," said a voice in my ear.

I jumped but managed not to shriek. Being wired was new to me, and I'd temporarily forgotten that Ben was watching from the control center disguised as a delivery van parked nearby.

"Sorry. Didn't mean to startle you," he added.

I stopped rubbing at my ear, even though the tiny transmitter planted within itched. Instead, I shoved my hands in my pockets and scanned the scene around me. The knowledge that so many eyes were watching made me feel fidgety, and because they were watching it seemed extra important not to fidget but to maintain an air of cool composure. Peter, especially, had been less than sanguine about Ben's plan to entrap Jake using me as bait, but I'd assured him I'd be fine with Ben and the colleagues he'd rounded up maintaining constant surveillance. Technically, this was still an off-the-books operation, as the powers that be seemed happy to blame Andrew Marcus for everything, but Ben had convinced a couple of his co-workers to help him out.

Of course, if we were going to entrap Jake, we also needed him to show up, and he seemed to be running late. I removed a hand from my pocket in order to check my watch.

"It's ten past twelve," said Ben's voice in my ear. I returned my hand to my pocket and resumed trying not to fidget.

A few more minutes passed before Ben spoke again. "Is that him? On the southwest corner? About to cross Canal?"

I checked out the southwest corner, squinting against the bright sunlight, but I saw nobody who even resembled Jake.

"Rachel, that's the southeast corner. Look to your right."

I could tell right from left, at least. This time my gaze landed on Jake, standing on the opposite corner and waiting for the light to change. He saw me and waved. In his weekend wear he blended right in with the tourists, smiling broadly beneath the rim of a blue baseball cap. I really didn't understand the appeal hats held for men who weren't losing their hair, but I'd have to get to the bottom of that on another day.

I plastered an equally broad smile on my own face as he loped across the street.

"Hey, there," he said warmly, as if he hadn't tried to kill me a few short days ago, and I submitted to a hug as if I didn't find it infuriating that he thought I was too stupid to realize that he'd tried to kill me. "You hungry?" he asked over the din of traffic.

I nodded. "Always."

"Good, me, too." I saw his eyes glance down at my hands, no doubt looking for my engagement ring. I'd left it off on purpose, thinking that if I could manage to flirt even a little bit I'd be more likely to puff up his ego while simultaneously loosening his tongue. And it was probably my imagination, but his smile seemed to take on a more cocky aspect once he'd ascertained the ring's absence. "There's a place I really like a block or so up Bowery. It's sort of a tourist trap, but the food is awesome."

"Awesome," I echoed. "What's it called?"

"The Golden Panda or Buddha's Garden or something like that. I can never keep these places straight."

"You don't know its name?"

"I'll know it when I see it," he said with confidence.

That was all well and good for Jake, but I would have preferred to be able to give Ben and his surveillance team a bit more to go on.

"So it's north of Canal on Bowery," I said, striving to sound as if I always liked to state my destination in casual conversation. Jake put a hand on my back as we turned up the street, and I tried not to think about cooties. It would be hard to entrap him if I let my hostility show. I needed to ease things along gently if I were going to get him to reveal the critical details proving that he and Annabel had carried out the attack on Dahlia.

"So what about that Mark Anders?" he said, his tone all jovial collegiality. "That was crazy, wasn't it?"

"Crazy," I agreed.

"I still can't get over what went down yesterday. And the way you tackled the guy—impressive stuff."

"It was nothing," I said, even though the places I'd landed were still sore. I could only imagine how poor Ben must feel.

"I didn't know you had it in you."

"I played football in high school," I said.

"Really? Oh, you're being sarcastic. Got it. Anyhow, it was

awesome." He moved his hand from my back to drape his arm casually over my shoulders. I had to force myself not to slap it away.

Jake continued on in this vein for another block, and I tried to keep up my end of the conversation while simultaneously sidestepping tourists and narrating our whereabouts. If you didn't know better, you would have mistaken us for just another couple in search of brunch on a lazy weekend day.

Then Jake's grip suddenly tightened around my shoulders.

Without warning, he pulled me into a small opening between two buildings, jerking my head roughly to one side.

"What are you do—" I started to ask.

But he clamped his hand over my mouth.

"Listen up," he said, propelling me along the narrow alley. His voice had completely lost its jovial tone. "Here's the deal. We're going for a little trip. And I really don't want to have to do anything that would leave any marks or bruises on you, so I suggest you cooperate."

Since he now had me in a headlock, I didn't really have much choice in the matter. I couldn't even open my mouth wide enough to bite at his hand, which was probably just as well given my concern about cooties. I did manage a sharp elbow to his ribs, but the only effect it had was to make Jake tighten the noose his arm had formed around my neck. I may not have been on the football team, but it definitely felt like Jake had put in some time on the wrestling squad.

The alley opened up into a small back lot, empty except for a Dumpster and a black Range Rover with tinted windows. A thin wisp of smoke trailed from its exhaust pipe.

The door to the back seat opened, and Jake shoved me inside.

"No—" I started to yell as soon as he'd removed his hand from my mouth.

But before I could get much noise out, another hand descended. An enormous diamond on the ring finger caught the light, confirming that the hand belonged to Annabel Gallagher just before she pressed a damp cloth over my face.

I smelled something both chemical and sweet.

And then I smelled nothing at all.

chapter thirty-five

Consciousness returned slowly. The black faded to charcoal and then to gray, and I became aware of voices and the hum of tires against pavement.

As far as I could tell, I was in the rear of the moving SUV. The seat had been folded down to create space for a prone body—namely, me—and I was lying on one plastic tarp while covered by another. I wanted to reach up a hand to push off the top sheet, but my arms were pinned behind my back. The creamy feel of silk twill around my wrists suggested that an Hermès scarf had been used to accomplish this, and when I tried to kick at the plastic with one foot the other foot came with it, which suggested that they were also tied together, although it was unclear if this had been done with an equally stylish and classy accessory.

The only silver lining was that Jake and I hadn't actually

made it to dim sum, because my head was throbbing and the accompanying nausea was sufficiently intense to make me glad that my stomach was empty.

In the front seat, Jake and Annabel were arguing.

"Please tell me you didn't charge the drop cloths on a credit card," Jake was saying.

"I never pay cash," Annabel replied. "Except at that manicure place on Madison. They don't accept American Express. Not even a platinum card. But they do a much better job than the place on Lexington."

"The drop cloths are to make sure that there's no trace evidence in the car." Jake sounded as if he was speaking through clenched teeth.

"I know that," she snapped. "And stop worrying. There won't be any trace evidence in the car. But there will be trace evidence on the drop cloths no matter what. She's lying all over them, spreading her DNA everywhere. We'll have to get rid of the drop cloths when we get rid of her, so stop making such a big deal about the stupid drop cloths already." I was still a bit spacey, and my first concern was that I was making a mess with my DNA and my second was for the scarf's well-being. It would be a shame to get rid of several hundred dollars' worth of designer silk.

"Yes, but if the drop cloths are ever found, they might be able to connect them to you because of the credit card records."

"Nobody will find them," Annabel said with confidence. "Why would anybody find them?"

"Even if they don't find them, it's a strange purchase for

you. Do you shop at the hardware store a lot? I mean, it's not exactly Barney's or Bergdorf's or any of your other usual spots. If anybody starts looking at your credit card receipts, that's the sort of thing that would stick out."

"Why would anybody look at my credit card receipts? You're being absurd."

"I'm not being absurd. And would you mind keeping your eyes on the road?"

"You are being absurd. And you had better not start in on my driving."

"I'm not saying anything about your driving. Except that you're supposed to watch the road."

"Would you like to get out and walk, Jake? Because that could be arranged."

The bickering continued while I took stock of my situation.

I was tied up in the back seat of a moving vehicle, and I was fairly certain that on previous occasions one of the people in the front seat had tried to kill Dahlia while the other person in the front seat had tried to kill me. It also seemed clear that they were now discussing logistics associated with how to more successfully commit murder, and, more specifically, how to more successfully murder me.

The casual observer might have concluded that this would be a good time to panic.

But I had no need to panic. Thanks to the handy transmitter in my ear, all I had to do was let Ben and his colleagues know where I was. Then they could swoop in and rescue me.

I just needed to make sure that I got Jake and Annabel to tell all before any swooping and rescuing occurred.

"I think she's awake," Jake said.

"Should we dose her again?"

"No. We'll need her awake to write the confession. Besides, the less chloroform we have to give her the better. I don't want any of it in her system if she's found."

"She's not going to be found. We'll weight her down too well for that."

"I hope not. But you always read about bodies washing up on shore—it's probably better to be safe than sorry." Jake raised his voice. "How are you doing back there, Rachel?"

"Just fine, thanks." I raised my voice to be heard from under the plastic.

"Glad to hear it."

"Uh, Jake? This might sound like a stupid question, but—"

"—there's no such thing as a stupid question, Rach."

"Do you have any idea how condescending you sound when you talk that way?" Annabel asked.

"I'm not being condescending. It's important to create an environment where people feel comfortable taking risks," Jake replied. He did sound condescending, and I disagreed with the premise that there were no stupid questions, even though it was something you heard people say a lot in professional services firms, but now didn't seem like a good time to disagree with him on either front.

"I have two questions, actually."

"Shoot," he said, and while I couldn't see him, I could picture his good-natured grin.

"Okay. Where are we going, and what are you planning on doing with me? Oh, and why? It would be good to know why. Although I guess that makes it three questions."

"We're on the Long Island Expressway, heading out to the Hamptons."

"Any special reason we're heading out to the Hamptons? It's a nice day and everything for March, but it's still not warm enough for the beach."

"We have some business to take care of out there. Nothing you need to worry about."

"Jake, just tell her already," interjected Annabel.

"No need to get her upset."

"She's probably figured out that she has a reason to be upset. You know, you just assume that any decent-looking woman is dumb and will believe anything you say. You've really become very sexist, and it's not an attractive quality," she said.

It occurred to me that helping to sow further dissension between my would-be killers might be beneficial. "It really isn't an attractive quality," I agreed. "He hides it really well, but once you get to know him—"

"—you find out that he's a chauvinistic pig. Jake, you're going to have to work on that."

"I am not a sexist," said Jake.

"Right," said Annabel sarcastically. If this was how they got along when they were having an illicit affair, I didn't hold out much hope for their prospects in a legitimate relationship, particularly since they were going to have to get by without a windfall from the Thunderbolt deal.

"I am not a sexist," Jake repeated, clearly straining to keep his voice even.

"Whatever," she replied.

"I'm not," he said again.

"Yes, Jake, we heard you the first two times," said Annabel. "Anyhow, Rachel, we feel bad about this, but we do need to get rid of you. So we're going out to Glenn's beach house. He keeps—whoops, I guess I mean kept, don't I? I'm still getting used to that. Glenn *kept* a boat there, and once it gets dark, we're going to take it out and drop you overboard. Might as well get some use out of the house and boat before that bitch Naomi takes over everything."

"Why are you telling her all that?" Jake asked.

"She has a right to know."

"What do you mean she has a right to know?"

"Don't use that tone with me."

"What tone?"

"*That* tone."

"It's not a tone."

"Well then what would you call it?"

I didn't want to be rude, but the squabbling was starting to get tedious, and the sooner I got the full story, the sooner the swooping and rescuing could begin, so I interrupted. "Uh, Jake? Annabel? I get what you're up to, but I'm still a bit confused as to why."

"Because Jake screwed up," said Annabel.

"I did not screw up," he protested.

"You screwed up," she insisted. "If it weren't for you, everybody would think Mark Anders or whatever that kid calls himself was the one who pushed Dahlia onto the tracks."

"We were setting Rachel up, not Mark," said Jake. "How was I supposed to know that I was giving him an alibi?"

"What do you mean, you gave Mark an alibi?" I asked.

"Wednesday morning. You got me worried that Dahlia was on to the Thunderbolt scam and that she'd tip you off, too. So we tried to solve both problems at once. Annabel dressed up like you and pushed Dahlia onto the tracks."

"I knew things were going too smoothly. First, Rachel's boyfriend spells out for you when she's going to be leaving the house."

"That was lucky. You usually take a cab in the morning, don't you, Rach? But Peter said you'd be getting off to a late start, and I figured you wouldn't be able to find one. And with Gallagher out of the picture, there was no reason for Dahlia to come in early, so it was a pretty safe bet when she'd be getting off the subway. Everything went perfectly, even better than if we'd actually killed Dahlia. She doesn't remember a thing."

"Except it didn't go perfectly," Annabel pointed out acidly.

"But everybody thinks Mark did it," I said. This wasn't exactly true, but everybody who had any decision-making power thought so—otherwise, I would have been having a much nicer day. "You have nothing to worry about. I don't understand what your problem is, much less what it has to do with me."

"Tell her, Jake. It's your fault."

"It's not my fault," he retorted.

"It is too your fault."

"Look, the only reason I had Mark come into the office early that day was to help with work we had to do to make sure that the Thunderbolt deal would get done on schedule. So if it's my fault, it's your fault, too."

"It's not my fault."

"Well, it's not my fault, either."

This time I decided to interrupt before they could get a good rhythm going. "Just to make sure I understand, Jake, you're saying that you made Mark come into work early on Wednesday, and now he has an alibi for when Annabel attacked Dahlia?"

"That's right," said Jake.

"And once the police get around to checking his alibi, they'll realize that somebody else must have attacked Dahlia?"

"Exactly," said Annabel. "So, we still need you to take the blame for that. We're going to need you to write a confession before we go out on the boat."

It was impolite of them to assume I'd be willing to take the blame, much less write out a confession, but the finer points of etiquette seemed to have escaped them, and now didn't seem like a productive time for a tutorial on manners. "But what was my motivation?" I asked instead. "Now that everybody knows I didn't kill Gallagher, why would they believe I wanted to attack Dahlia? It's not like I was worried that she knew something incriminating about me or anything I'd done."

"That's easy," said Jake. "You were in love with me, and

you thought I was interested in Dahlia, and you were jealous. So you attacked her, but now you know you'll be found
out, and you can't live with yourself anymore, and you can't
have me, so you're going to write a confession and then
drown yourself."

It took me a moment to absorb this one, and when I did,
it rendered me nearly speechless.

"You've—what—but—"

The nerve of the guy! Not to mention the out-of-
control ego.

"Are you insane?" I finally managed to spit out.

"It's not insane," said Annabel. "I mean, he has his issues,
but you have to admit he's a good-looking guy."

"The chicks dig me," Jake agreed. "It's incredible the
way they just eat up the entire 'I'm-not-so-good-at-
relationships' pathetic loser thing."

"Grow up," said Annabel in disgust. *"Chicks?"*

"I've already planted a few rumors that things have been
rocky with your fiancé," added Jake. "And people know
that we've been spending a lot of time together. And nobody would be surprised if they heard I was into Dahlia—
have you seen the rack on her?"

"That's so juvenile," said Annabel.

"What's juvenile?"

"You are! Did you really just refer to a woman's breasts
as 'a rack'? I know more sophisticated thirteen-year-olds."

"Maybe you should have stuck with Gallagher. Nobody
would ever mistake him for anything less than middle-
aged," said Jake.

"Maybe I should have," she said.

"Maybe you should have," he repeated.

"Shut up."

"You shut up."

"No, you shut up."

I was glad about the transmitter and my imminent deliverance, because it would have been truly tragic for my last hours on earth to be so lacking in witty banter. And I had all of the information I needed. It was time for the swooping and rescuing to begin.

"Ben?" I whispered as Jake and Annabel continued to argue in the front seat.

I waited for the voice in my ear to reply.

"You got all that, right, Ben?"

Nothing.

"Ben?" I whispered again.

And still nothing.

Then I noticed that despite the throbbing in my head and the queasiness in my stomach and the awkward position my arms were in and the way my neck still ached from Jake's headlock, one body part felt pretty good.

My ear no longer itched.

chapter thirty-six

The transmitter was gone.

I briefly tried to convince myself that perhaps that it had fallen out of my ear and attached itself to a piece of clothing or tangled itself in my hair, in which case, Ben would have been able to continue monitoring the conversation even if I was unable to hear anything from his end. But the continued absence of Ben or any type of rescue effort didn't do much to bolster my hopes. And then Jake put the nail in the coffin of my hopes.

"Hey, Rach. You didn't spend your own money on that transmitter thing, did you? Because we threw it out the window somewhere on Canal Street. Sorry about that."

I pictured the small, ticklike button lying on the dirty pavement and tried not to groan.

The transmitter was completely gone. And I was completely screwed.

I was alone, outnumbered and defenseless, and I was fairly confident that the waters off Bridgehampton would be less than balmy. Not that I'd last very long once overboard. I could only hope that sharks migrated south in the winter like birds.

Nobody would be coming to rescue me. Nobody knew what had happened, or where I was, or what Jake and Annabel had planned for me, or why they had planned it in the first place.

I should have known better than to rely on anyone else.

It was up to me, and only me, to save myself.

This realization drained the last of my good humor. Jake and Annabel were still playing their little game of You-Shut-Up/No-You-Shut-Up in the front seat, but I'd had enough.

"Why don't you *both* shut up!" I bellowed.

"Hey, Rach. There's nothing to gain by getting all worked up," said Jake.

"There's nothing to gain by killing me," I snapped back. "Nobody—nobody—would believe that I killed myself over you, you conceited ass."

Annabel chimed in. "You are conceited, Jake. I mean, I'm not worried that we won't be able to put the whole thing over, but your ego is getting sort of bloated."

Divide and conquer, I thought, as they bickered over whether or not Jake was conceited. I would use my keen wit to derail their plan. The fact that the two of them seemed headed for couple's therapy at a rapid clip could only work in my favor. My mind raced as I tried to come up with a reason for Annabel to join me in ganging up on

Jake, or any reason I could put forth to dissuade them from their current path.

But it was as if they could read my thoughts.

"You have to understand, Rach. It's nothing personal," said Jake after he and Annabel had agreed to table the conceitedness issue. "We spent a lot of time thinking this through, and there's just no other alternative."

"He's right, Rachel. You have to take the fall for the Dahlia thing. There's no other way. It's either you or me, and I'm going to have to go with you."

"That's so typical of you, Annabel, to look at it that way. Killing Rachel is something *we* need to do for *our* future. It's not just about you. I may be conceited, but you're selfish," Jake said.

As they launched into heated debate over whether Annabel was more selfish than Jake was conceited, I turned my attention to my hands and feet. If reason was out, maybe I could attempt physical persuasion. If I could only untie myself, then I'd be able to take them by surprise and overpower them somehow. There had to be a weapon of some sort here in the back seat with me, a tire iron or golf club or handy meat cleaver I could put to good use.

But no matter how I wiggled and squirmed, I couldn't free my hands from the knotted silk scarf, and I knew better than to think that anything that expensive would simply tear and give way. The odds of physically persuading Jake and Annabel not to kill me seemed about as inauspicious as the odds of reasoning with them. They'd probably have to untie me so I could write out whatever fake confession they

wanted me to write out, but I doubted that they'd be careless enough for me to make my escape then.

"Slow down," Jake warned Annabel in the front seat. "You
don't want to miss the turnoff."

"I'm not going to miss the turnoff."

"You're in the wrong lane. You need to start getting over."

"The exit's not for another two miles."

"You're still in the wrong lane."

The car swerved to the right. "Happy now?"

"Happier, yes. But you should use your blinker when you
switch lanes."

"There's hardly anybody else on the road! Who cares if
I use the blinker?"

I scanned through my options again, hoping against hope
that I'd missed something. But I wasn't coming up with
anything viable.

In fact, I was coming up with nothing.

The car's pace slowed as Annabel turned off the highway.
It seemed wrong that when I actually wanted to go to the
beach, traffic was a nightmare, but when I had no interest
in arriving there we just cruised right along.

I sighed. It was looking like I should start resigning myself to a cold and watery death. A certain fatalism washed
over me. I found myself wondering if there was anything
embarrassing at my home or office, any items that I wouldn't
want discovered by the unfortunate person charged with
clearing out my belongings. Not that it really mattered,
since I couldn't be embarrassed when I was dead, but I
didn't want to tarnish the memories of me that Peter and

my family and friends would otherwise cherish. And I hoped there would be good food at the reception after my funeral. I'd always been a big fan of the pig in a blanket, and while I recognized that some might consider it an inappropriate funeral dish, I personally believed it was suitable for any occasion. Although, it was a dish best served with champagne, and not the cheap stuff, either. I hoped that somebody would spring for something nice and dry and bubbly.

"The light's turning red," said Jake.

"It still looks yellow to me," Annabel replied.

"This would be a very bad time to get pulled over for running a red light."

"Geez, Grandma," Annabel grumbled, but the car came to a stop.

"I'd feel a lot safer with my grandmother behind the wheel."

"How long is this light, anyway?"

"What's your hurry? We can't kill her until after dark. We have plenty of—"

I was weighing the relative merits of pigs in a blanket and miniquiches when I briefly registered the sound of a car engine accelerating behind us.

Then Jake's words were lost in the roar of metal crashing into metal.

chapter thirty-seven

The impact threw me forward, my head collided with the back of the driver's seat, and the sunny afternoon gave way to shooting silver stars.

The car skidded some distance and then crashed into an unyielding object. My head hit the back of the driver's seat again.

I heard a voice cry out. It could have been mine, or it could have been Annabel's—it could even have been Jake's, taking on a strangely soprano note—but it was impossible to tell over the whoosh of exploding air bags. Not that there were air bags in the back seat—my safety hadn't been of primary concern to the happy couple in the front.

I struggled up into a sitting position, which took significantly more abdominal strength than I would have guessed I had, New Year's resolutions regarding personal trainers notwithstanding. Through the haze of shooting silver stars,

I managed to ascertain that the air bags had pinned both Jake and Annabel to their seats, effectively immobilizing them. Police sirens sounded in the distance.

I registered a fleeting moment of joy. My would-be killers had been thwarted, I wouldn't be swimming with the fishes any time soon, and I'd learned that I should leave very specific instructions in my will regarding hors d'oeuvres to be served at my funeral.

Then I blacked out completely.

When I came to, I heard Peter's voice nearby, in muted conversation with other, unfamiliar voices.

My first thought was to wonder what he was doing there. It was with a mix of relief, affection and shame that I realized I'd been a little quick to assume I'd been left so thoroughly on my own. I hadn't been alone, after all. There was someone I could rely on. And he'd turned out to be very reliable.

My second thought was to wonder how he'd gotten there. Then I opened my eyes and took a good look around.

My third thought was to hope that Luisa's insurance covered this sort of thing.

It was late by the time we were able to hitch a ride back to the city, and I'd lost track of how many law enforcement agencies had questioned us, much less which agency was actually providing our transportation. However, I appreciated that the officers in the front seat seemed comfortable leaving us to our own devices in the back seat. That the front and back seats were separated by a bulletproof glass panel also helped secure our privacy, although I found the lack of handles on the doors a bit discomfiting, especially given how recently I'd been entrapped in another moving vehicle.

"How did you know?" I asked Peter. "Jake said they tossed the transmitter out on Canal Street."

"I was worried that everyone was underestimating Jake, and I wanted to make sure you had more backup than the transmitter. I was in Luisa's car just below Canal as you were waiting for him."

"You found parking?" This was almost more impressive than the way in which he'd saved my life.

"I got there early—I left the apartment right after you left to meet Ben—and I circled the block. It took awhile, but eventually a space with a good view of the corner opened up."

"And then you trailed us up the street? And you saw what happened? You saw Jake pull me into that alley?"

"The nerve of that guy."

"But—how did you follow us? How did you know where to find me?"

"A handy little thing I like to call a map," he said with a smile. "I'd been studying it while I was waiting, and I knew where that alley led. I got there just as the Range Rover pulled out, and I could see Jake and Annabel in the front. I figured they wouldn't have bothered with the car if they were going to leave you in the alley, so I followed them. Before I knew it, we were over the Manhattan Bridge and on the highway. I thought I'd keep the car in sight and call the police."

"Didn't your phone work?"

"I'm an idiot—I didn't even have it with me. I'd left it in the apartment when I sneaked out on Thursday, and I forgot all about it this morning."

"So you had to improvise."

"Yes," he said. "I had to improvise." The warm chocolate of his eyes was now set off by purplish bruising from where the airbags in the BMW had exploded in his face. Ben wasn't going to be the only one with a black eye in the morning.

"You know, nobody's ever going to lend us a car again."

"Who needs a car when you live in Manhattan?"

We would find out later that Luisa's car was indeed insured; regardless, she made it very clear that neither Peter nor I was ever authorized to drive one of her vehicles again.

"Would you rather that Peter hadn't done anything? That he'd saved your precious car but let Jake and Annabel kill me?" I asked her.

"I don't know if you want me to answer that question," she replied.

I also found out that all of my friends being in town the same week wasn't a fortunate coincidence but had occurred purely by design: they'd been planning a surprise engagement party for Peter and me.

Of course, I'd ruined everything by skipping town the night before the party, but they seemed willing to forgive me.

"I just don't know when we're going to be able to get another date on the calendar," said Jane. "Between the baby and everyone's schedules, it's going to be hard. And we really wanted it to be a surprise."

"It was a surprise," I said. "I had no idea that you were planning anything. So it worked. Thank you."

"Surprising you isn't the same thing as having a party, though. Maybe we can do a bridal shower," suggested Emma. "Or a joint baby and bridal shower for Jane and Rachel together. That could be fun."

"How would that be fun?" asked Hilary. "Have you ever even been to a shower?"

I probably took more pleasure than was seemly in helping Ben put together his case against Nicholas Perry and Senator Brisbane and in testifying against Jake and Annabel. Annabel's new outfits were far less becoming than her usual selections from Prada and Gucci, but orange is a difficult color for blondes to wear well.

I took less pleasure in the statements I had to make about Andrew Marcus. He might have been a coldblooded killer, but he'd killed to avenge his family, which seemed like a more noble purpose than the money that had motivated the various other wrong-doers involved. I also appreciated the way he'd prevented Jake from shooting me at the boat basin, not to mention the thorough efficiency with which he'd completed his work on the Thunderbolt deal. Good associates were hard to find.

And I could have used a good associate, because I was soon busy at work again, helping Frank Kryzluk and the Thunderbolt board of directors put together an employee buyout of the company. There was a McDonald's at the

Pittsburgh Airport, but even though the flight from New York took over an hour, it didn't really count as a road trip, so I couldn't justify stopping there.

It was close to midnight by the time we reached my apartment building that Sunday night. The doorman helped us out of the squad car that had chauffeured us home from the Hamptons with an admirable lack of comment. I slumped against Peter in the elevator, my eyes closed and practically asleep on my feet. It had been a long day. In fact, it had been a long week.

"Come on," he said as the elevator doors parted.

I opened my eyes.

"Peter, we're on the wrong floor." The little brass plate said sixteen, not fifteen.

"No, we're not." He bent and retrieved a key from under the door mat in front of 16A.

"Peter, you can't just take somebody else's key like that. And this is the apartment right upstairs from mine. Who-ever lives here can make things pretty miserable for us if we piss them off. Stomping around, dragging things, playing loud music. It can get ugly."

He ignored me and turned the key in the door.

"Peter, this really isn't funny. It's dangerous to upset your upstairs neighbors."

He started to pocket the key, and then he caught him-self. "We'll need to make a copy of this for you."

"Have you not had enough interaction with law enforce-ment agencies today?"

"Come here," he said, propping the door open with his foot.

"What are you doing—" I started to ask. Then he picked me up.

"It's a little premature, but I'm carrying you over the threshold."

"Of somebody else's apartment."

"No, it's ours."

"What?"

"I bought it. It's ours. And we can build a staircase down to your apartment. I already checked with an architect."

"How did you—I mean, when did you—" Was this what all of his phone calls had been about? And why he'd been here instead of at his office in the middle of the day?

"Shh," he said.

And he carried me over the threshold.

On Sale December

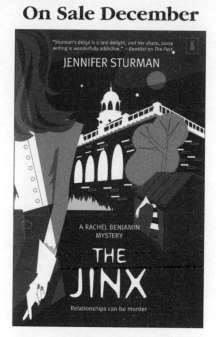

"Sturman's debut is a rare delight, and her sharp, sassy writing is wonderfully addictive." —*Booklist* on *The Pact*

JENNIFER STURMAN

A RACHEL BENJAMIN MYSTERY

THE JINX

Relationships can be murder

THE JINX
by Jennifer Sturman

The much-anticipated sequel to THE PACT!

Rachel Benjamin finally has it all—a great boyfriend
and an exciting career. But when trouble strikes and
Rachel must take on the role of Miss Marple again,
she wonders if she jinxed everything just when she
stopped worrying about jinxing things.

Available wherever
trade paperbacks
are sold.

RED DRESS INK
TM

The Pact

by Jennifer Sturman

A mystery for anyone who has ever
hated a friend's boyfriend

Rachel Benjamin and her friends aren't looking forward to Emma's wedding. The groom is a rat, and
nobody can understand what Emma sees in him.
So when he turns up dead on the morning of the
ceremony, no one in the wedding party is all that
upset. Is it possible that one of the five best friends
took a pact they made in university too far?

More great reads from international
bestselling author Sarah Mlynowski

As Seen on TV

Sunny Langstein has done what every modern-day
twenty-four-year-old shouldn't do. She's left her life
in Florida to move in with her boyfriend in
Manhattan. But don't judge Sunny yet, because
like any smart woman she has an ulterior motive—
to star on *Party Girls,* the latest reality-television
show. Here's the catch—*Party Girls* have to be
single. Free designer clothes and stardom versus
life with her boyfriend. What's a girl to do?

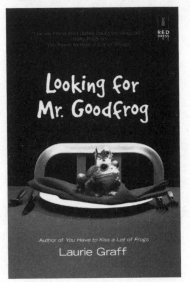

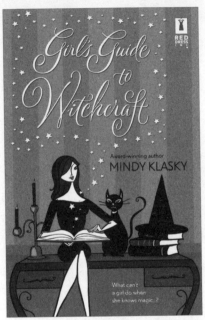